THE TAXI QUEUE

Janet Davey is the author of *English Correspondence* (2003) and *First Aid* (2004). She lives in London.

F

ALSO BY JANET DAVEY

English Correspondence
First Aid

JANET DAVEY

The Taxi Queue

VINTAGE BOOKS
London

Published by Vintage 2008

2 4 6 8 10 9 7 5 3 1

First published in Great Britain in 2007 by Chatto & Windus

Vintage
Random House, 20 Vauxhall Bridge Road,
London SW1V 2SA

www.vintage-books.co.uk

Addresses for companies within The Random House Group Limited can be found at: www.randomhouse.co.uk/offices.htm

The Random House Group Limited Reg. No. 954009

A CIP catalogue record for this book is available from the British Library

ISBN 9780099506966

The Random House Group Limited supports The Forest Stewardship Council (FSC), the leading international forest certification organisation. All our titles that are printed on Greenpeace approved FSC certified paper carry the FSC logo. Our paper procurement policy can be found at: www.rbooks.co.uk/environment

Printed and bound in Great Britain by
CPI Bookmarque, Croydon, CR0 4TD

TO MY SISTER, ELIZABETH

One

1

When the other passengers stood up and bunched in the aisle to leave the train at London, Paddington, Abe Rivers stayed put. What was the rush? People streamed past the windows and then they were gone. Abe waited. He waited until the electronic indicator at the end of the carriage stopped rolling off destinations and showed 'EMPTY TO DEPOT'. Then the lights went out. Abe sidled between the abandoned seats and stepped off the train. The doors slid shut behind him. As he walked towards the ticket barrier, along the cold echoey platform, he could see people in the distance penned up on the station concourse. Only the trains seemed at liberty. They departed, one after another, for their own good, to rest in sidings and sheds.

Moving into the crowd, Abe was rammed by a man in a luminous orange safety jacket and two women – arm in arm for maximum aggression – who formed an advancing wall. They were already suspicious of the revised winter timetable. Now it had vaporised. The departures board was blank. Using party-going cleavage, under fake fur, the women shoved the safety jacket in case the man inside worked for the railways and should have been out sweeping snow from the track. They shoved at Abe because he was in their way and should never have been born. They abused their country and the Mayor of London with mouths wide open, showing the bumps on their tongues and dispensing alcoholic fumes. Abe felt sickeningly hot. Tipping his head back to gain more air, he noticed a dingy mist, formed by the covering of snow on the station roof, hanging low under its arch, and imagined it descending. Until the crowd loosened enough for him to be able to squeeze through, he breathed deeply and tried to keep his nostrils out of the women's hair. Once he could feel some give in the bodies, he edged his way to the exit, sidestepping, finding a random path, as water finds a way through rocks.

Outside, Abe ran into the taxi queue – another mass of people but differently configured. They stretched into a line that vanished into the distance. Iverdale Road, where Abe lived, was a few miles away, on the Willesden side of Kensal Rise. Usually he caught a bus but tonight the buses would be full; he preferred to walk. He pushed past the queue and set off up the slope towards Eastbourne Terrace. As he emerged from the shelter of the station canopy, he took a hat out of one of his pockets and pulled it down firmly over his hair. At least his head would be warm. His skinny-fitting coat was fashionable enough but light as a graze. He tightened the knot in his scarf and tilted his head, letting the flakes fall full on his face. He felt as if he had rubbed a dark patch in a steamy window and was seeing winter for the first time. He had always enjoyed snow. He carried on walking. Trudging.

Somewhere along Eastbourne Terrace, Abe reached the far end of the taxi queue. He registered the person in this position, as he noticed the ultimate place names on the tube lines – now just names – currently inaccessible. Someone has to be last, he thought. The man was about forty – older than Abe – conventionally dressed. He was carrying a corporate golfing umbrella which, like the flag of a recently invented country, represented something, though no one knew what. Abe disliked corporate golfing umbrellas but the way the man was standing – a separateness that was hard to define, but which Abe had a nose for – made him take a second look at the face underneath. In the shadow, he caught something in the expression that appealed to him – a sense of loneliness, more or less under control, that didn't just come from being at the end of the line. The man saw Abe looking and returned the glance. Abe walked a few paces on and came back. He joined the queue.

After a few minutes the man said, 'People ahead seem to be organising cab shares. I'm going to Sudbury Hill. Is that any good to you?'

'That's cool,' Abe said. 'Thanks.' He knocked the snow off his wet shoes and put his hands in his pockets. Taxis were turning down the ramp sporadically, not in a regular stream, their headlamps and 'for hire' lights hazy in the snow.

'We've only just got through Christmas and New Year,' the man said. 'Now another shutdown.'

'Yeah, it's part of a plot.'

'Do you work near here?' the man asked.

'No. Reading. Reverse commute. But I'm thinking of leaving.' Abe mentioned the name of a health insurance company. He was on the marketing side, he said.

The man said he had come from a client meeting in the new Paddington Basin development. He worked for a City-based firm of chartered accountants. His voice was matter-of-fact but friendly.

'Good meeting?' Abe asked.

'Not too many surprises.'

The two of them waited without speaking again; falling into a listless rhythm of standing still, moving a couple of metres, stopping again. From time to time, announcements from inside the station boomed – though indistinctly. Abe's phone was silent and Abe went off into a dreamlike state partly induced by the weather. After about half an hour, they were under the station canopy and in another twenty minutes at the head of the queue. Other people were now behind – proxies, it seemed, for all those who had previously been in front – clothed in the same uncertain colours under the murky light. A taxi pulled up.

'Our turn,' Abe said, opening the taxi door.

The man, a woman and Abe got in – in that order. Abe was unprepared for the woman but she sat down quickly and was firm about wanting to be dropped off at Perivale. She smelled rather strongly of fresh musky scent as if she had sprayed herself shortly before leaving the office. The man and the woman settled next to each other on the bench seat, Abe facing them. He glanced from one to the other – the brief-cases resting on the knees, the leather gloves placed on top. He had thought he and the man had something in common but looking at the matching arrangement and the expensive black coats, Abe wondered if he had guessed wrong. The other two might start discussing offshore funds and *he* would be discounted. The man seemed to avoid meeting his eyes. Abe wrapped his own thin coat with its sharp lapels more tightly round himself. He pulled off his beanie hat and shook out his hair. He stared out of the window.

The woman snapped her phone open and was then on it constantly – talking dates and arrangements, checking whether the next morning's flights to New York would take off. When they crossed the North Circular she made a call to say she was on her way home. Whoever she was speaking to must have passed her to a child because she changed her voice. Poor kid, Abe thought. Shortly afterwards, the taxi driver called through the hatch and said he wasn't going to risk the side streets, he would only stop on the main road. The woman leant forward, filling up the space with her coat. A sleeve brushed Abe's cheek. He batted it out of the way but the woman remained close, pitched towards the hatch, while she told the driver that she would get out after the next junction. She sat back. She squeezed her hands into the gloves, moulding the leather over her rings. The taxi pulled across two lines of slow-moving traffic to the inside lane and stopped by the forecourt of a petrol station, blocking the exit. The woman got out and walked away. They set off again. Abe moved across to the bench seat.

He felt the warmth left behind by the woman and shifted slightly.

'Cheapskate,' Abe said.

'Yes. Odd behaviour.' The man looked at him. Abe stretched out his legs and put his hands behind his head. The man seemed to relax. It was quiet in the cab without the woman, though her scent persisted. In the darkness, illuminated on and off by slow flashes of light from oncoming headlamps, Abe noticed the man's shoes – highly polished, resistant to water – the trousers with an apparently weatherproof crease, the knuckles of his hands firm and pale, as they rested on the briefcase. The snow on their clothes had lost its frostiness and drips from the umbrella were making a pool on the floor.

As they drove further into the suburbs the temperature fell. The office blocks and parades of shops were left behind. There were only houses now; rows of thirties semis that gave way to larger properties set further apart from each other, their roofs and gardens thickly white. The street lamps became sporadic. The road, which had been straight and wide, began to curve and rise. The taxi driver dropped his speed to ten miles per hour and kept changing gear – but he carried on driving. Abe could feel the covering of snow on the road. There was padding beneath them. The wheel paths of other vehicles were no longer present. They struggled on upwards.

The taxi stopped abruptly and the driver pulled down the sliding window between his cab and the carriage. He looked over his shoulder, moving his upper body round with his head, to show that the stopping was permanent. He said he wouldn't go any further. They'd have to get out and walk it. Abe's companion said that that was all right for him, his house wasn't far away. He turned to Abe, 'But what about you?' Abe said he lived in Harrow.

'Whereabouts?' the driver said, interrupting.

Although he didn't fully understand the geography of places

further out west and had never been to any of them, Abe knew, more or less, that starting from Paddington, Perivale was west of Kensal Rise where he lived, Sudbury, where they were heading for, was beyond Perivale, and Harrow was right out of London, almost in the country and perched on a hill.

'On the Hill,' Abe said.

'Forget it, mate. It'll be like Switzerland up there,' the taxi driver said.

So the man offered to put Abe up for the night.

'I'm Abe,' Abe said, as the taxi turned in the road. The cab engine chugged in the silence and the tail lights glowed red against the snow. Abe bent down to tuck the bottom of his trousers into his socks.

'Richard,' the man said. He moved his arm so that his umbrella was over Abe but Abe shook his head. He distrusted umbrellas; he didn't want his eye poked out. The taxi went back down the hill and the chugging grew faint. The two men began to walk. They were much the same height, both long-legged, but Abe had a lazier, more loping style of walking. The snow was crunchy but not slippery and creaked as they stepped into it.

'I'm really grateful,' Abe said. He was conscious of his voice in the quiet.

'This wasn't forecast,' Richard said. Neither of them had mentioned the weather. It was as if they had, until then, made a pact to disregard it.

'It would have taken me a long time to walk home,' Abe said.

'Anyone there who'll be worrying about you?'

'No. My sister won't worry. I share a house with my sister.'

'Sounds a good arrangement.' Richard paused. 'Is it?'

'Suits me,' Abe said. 'We moved in together a couple of months ago.'

'What's she called?'

'Kirsty. Kirsty Rivers. We're both Rivers.'

'Abe and Kirsty.' Richard tried the combination. 'Does anyone call you Abraham?' he asked, though the change was no better.

'Just Abe.'

'Father of many nations,' Richard said, as if Abe hadn't replied.

'Probably not. Not yet, anyway. It's a family name. My grandad's.'

'Continuity's good,' Richard said.

'Every now and then,' Abe said.

They carried on walking up the looped bends of the hill. They had got used to not talking in the time they had spent together but lapsing into silence out of doors felt less manageable, more awkward. On each side of the road were tall, bare-branched trees. There were mysterious curlicued gates, rewritten in white, but the houses, if they existed, had been built out of sight of passers-by.

Richard indicated that they should turn off. With the edge of the kerbs buried, the side road gave the illusion of a country lane. Space was measured differently in falling snow. Newish detached houses began to occur at regular intervals, faintly ridiculous in the winter landscape, four-square under pitched roofs, with wide porches made up of two pillars and a triangular pediment. The only asymmetries were the double garages to the side of each house. The gardens were spacious in their tidy whiteness.

'The house isn't far now,' Richard said. 'The tree ahead, the silver fir. That's in the drive.'

2

The frontage was open, without gates or hedges. The downstairs windows were dark, behind half-closed curtains, but a light that was on in the hall beamed through the blurred glass in the front door and out on to the snow. There was no visible path to the house but Richard approached as if there were one, walking to a point opposite the front door and making a right-angled turn. Abe took the same route, making his own footprints. A bulb at the top of a miniature lamp-post came on as they passed. Richard collapsed his umbrella and propped it against the wall of the porch. He put his hand in his pocket for his keys. He and Abe both stamped their feet simultaneously, to shake off loose snow. Richard opened the door and set the house alarm bleeping. He went across to a panel and punched in four numbers. Abe hung back politely in the doorway and looked away, as if he were waiting to use a bank cashpoint.

'It's all right, Abe, come in, you can close the door,' Richard said.

The hall was very warm and smelled of new carpet. Everything was neatly arranged in the spaces between closed doors. Radiators were concealed behind polished mahogany grilles and matching console tables stood facing them. The house was as silent as the road but with a shut-in kind of silence, as though it were sealed. The snow that clung to them seemed an impertinence – something wild that had been let in. Abe knelt down and took off his shoes.

'We'll go in the kitchen,' Richard said. 'I'll put our wet things in the utility room.'

Abe stood up. If he had arrived blindfold he wouldn't, once the blindfold was off, have known where he was. He might have guessed a lobby to private consulting rooms or a small new hotel. The interior had an impersonality and neatness he couldn't place. There was nothing that matched his notion of home. He followed Richard along a passage that led from the hall. A staircase was tucked round the corner. The carpet flowed upwards. Abe glanced at the dark hollow at the top where the steps disappeared into shadow. Bedrooms presumably – but he had no view of what was up there or what the layout might be.

Richard opened a door at the end of the passage and switched on a light. 'We live in here,' he said. 'I sometimes wonder why I bothered to buy a house with reception rooms. We hardly ever go in them.'

Abe blinked. The kitchen was a family room, sparklingly lit – equipped with giant floor cushions, plastic stacking boxes, television, computer – and backed by walls of sleek-looking cupboards and appliances. The main impression, though, was of space – stretches of uncluttered wooden floor. Abe started to peel off his hat, coat and scarf.

'Here, give them to me.' Richard took the wet clothes, one by one, as Abe removed them. The pull-on hat, the skimpy coat that weighed too little, the long nubbly scarf. For the first time Abe saw Richard clearly, face on; the mix of regularity and restlessness that had attracted him – it hadn't been a trick of the light. The two men looked at one another. Their gestures of giving and taking seemed to be in slow motion, almost exaggerated.

Richard bore the clothes away through a door on the far side of the kitchen. Abe wandered round the room, wearing the suit he always wore on work days: baggy trousers, slightly nipped-in jacket. 'Coal' was the name of the colour. He pulled at the damp ends of his hair.

What was left of the family was on the cork noticeboard. Abe examined it. Two little dark-haired girls in a paddling pool. The same again, but taller, side by side, wearing oversized sunglasses and staring at the camera. And again, dressed up for Hallowe'en in witches' hats and masks. Paintings. Collages. Home-made cards sprinkled with glitter. Swimming. Fun French. Gym Club. Bible Bus, a list of dates and addresses headed 'Prayer, Praise and Pasta'.

Richard reappeared. Abe turned away from the noticeboard. He turned deliberately. He didn't pretend he hadn't been looking at it. Richard came across to him. He touched Abe's arm and leant forward towards him. Without exerting pressure, he kissed Abe on the mouth. He had startled himself. Abe saw that in his eyes – the pinpoints of surprise in the pupils. Richard cleared his throat. 'Right,' he said, after a short pause that lasted longer than the kiss. He walked to the fridge and opened the door. 'Vivienne's left me all these meals marked up. What's today? Wednesday? Fish pie. Is that all right for you? We'll have Thursday's as well, or there won't be enough. Vegetable cannelloni. They'll go together all right, won't they? And some wine. Definitely wine.'

Richard picked up a towel and rubbed his hair, until soft tufts of it stood up. He took off his jacket and placed it over the back of a chair. From the knee down his trousers were wet and furrowed, the crease still holding up. The fridge behind him was chock-full, so crammed that its internal light was masked and everything inside looked shadowy. Suddenly he noticed that the door was wide open and began to rummage inside. He was unaware of Abe staring at him.

'Prayer, Praise and Pasta,' Abe said. 'Do your girls like that?' He said it to be friendly.

Richard straightened up. He looked, for a second, taken aback by Abe's question. 'It's more a grown-up thing,' he said. 'We take it in turns to go to each other's houses. Vivienne's good about all that. PP and P. Actually, the girls can't eat pasta. They're allergic to wheat.'

'I'm interested in religion,' Abe said.

'Religion,' Richard repeated as if it were a strange and perplexing word. He paused. 'Faith, I suppose, is what Vivienne would call it. What she'd say we – *had*.' He shut the fridge door without having taken anything out. He seemed undecided.

'Yes. Faith,' Abe said. 'Whatever. My mother's started one up.'

'She has?'

'Well, not started from scratch. More revived an old one. She does chanting.'

'Good heavens.'

'Egyptian. It seemed wrong to let all that stuff lie around unused,' Abe said. 'I'm going to make her a website. I'll give you the card I made, if you like. You can keep it.' His mother had given him *The Egyptian Book of the Dead* as part of his Christmas present, but he hadn't made much headway with it. There was one part of the book that he liked, though; it hovered on the edge of his thoughts. After death, a person had to give an account of his life and what counted was not what he had or had not done, but how truthful the account was. The person's heart was weighed against truth. Abe put his hand in his top pocket and laid a small rectangular card on the table. 'Truth's a feather,' he said. 'That's why that feather's on it.'

Richard walked over to the table and picked up the card. He looked at it and laid it down again carefully. 'I'm a bit out of my depth on this one, I'm afraid, but thank you very much.'

'My mum sings – and my sister,' Abe said.

'What's your sort of music?' Richard asked.

Abe hesitated. He was a bit allergic to older people discussing their favourite albums. He hoped Richard wouldn't go down that path. 'Ba-roque,' he said, with a hint of challenge. He had never used the word before. He left the very shortest pause between the two syllables.

‘Is that something I should know about?’ Richard said, cautiously.

Abe shrugged his shoulders. ‘It depends,’ he said. ‘Been around a while.’

Richard seemed as if he might ask another question. He ran his hand up and down the side of his face, as if testing his shaving, then he nodded and went back to the fridge and took out two dishes.

‘Where are they, Vivienne and the girls?’ Abe asked.

‘France. Skiing,’ Richard said. ‘I’m not a skier. Are you?’

Abe shook his head.

‘I never got the hang of it. To be truthful I’m afraid of falling.’ Richard stood, holding a dish in either hand, poised like a pair of scales.

Abe went across and took them from him. ‘Do the girls go out on their own?’ he asked, going to the microwave oven and opening the door.

‘No, not yet. They’re too young for that,’ Richard said.

Abe adjusted the rack inside the oven and inserted the dishes. ‘I had this idea when I was about twelve that I’d choose a tube station where I’d never been, go there and see what was going on. I went to Chalk Farm. I knew it wasn’t country but I was expecting, from the name, that it might be different from London. Somewhere you could get real cider or magic mushrooms. Fresh eggs. I can remember expecting eggs. Pale – like chalk. Some rubbish. I thought I might bring a present back for my mum.’

‘They haven’t been anywhere on their own yet – apart from sleepovers and we try to keep them to a minimum,’ Richard said.

‘Why’s that?’ Abe punched in a number and pressed the start button.

‘Too many sweets after lights out,’ Richard said. ‘They get hyper.’

‘Hyper? That’s good isn’t it?’ Abe said. ‘Being hyper? Part of the fun. I’d like kids one day. I like kids.’

Richard gave him a strange look. 'But not yet.'

'No. That's on hold.'

'Where else did you go?' Richard asked. 'On your mystery tours.'

'I only did it the once. There wasn't the same romance. I was left with the edges of the tube map. And weird places.'

Richard smiled. 'Bounds Green,' he said. 'I've always been fascinated by that name.'

'You might be disappointed. But try it,' Abe said. He slid on to the bench seating on one side of the table and sat down. He propped a cushion behind his head and leant back against the wall. Feathers, not foam, he thought. He felt happy: not energised or wanting to make plans, but peaceful. Richard was very trusting, very hospitable. This calmed Abe. He felt the rushing of the week had stopped and need not start again. On the other side of the kitchen Richard was opening a bottle and pouring red wine into two large, solid-looking glasses, splashing it in until the glasses were full and the bottle half empty. The fish pie was starting to smell good. Richard was walking towards him. Abe held out his hand. Richard put one of the glasses into it.

'Cheers,' Abe said and smiled. He didn't think he'd misjudged the situation.

Outside, the snow carried on falling, taking to itself the burden of movement.

3

Neil Rivers had died the previous summer and left Abe and Kirsty his house in Kensal Rise. He had never lived with his children. Neil Rivers had been a photographer once, momentarily famous, though there was no evidence of his work in 105 Iverdale Road – not even a copy of his celebrated poster. Over thirty years before his death, he had taken a picture of a girl leaning over Waterloo Bridge. Her hair flopped in a blonde sheet and her legs, under a micro-skirt, came up to the parapet. The image was classy; set at night, with a streak of dawn in the east that seemed more apocalyptic than hopeful. It still turned up in books about the seventies. The girl, Tamsin Spira, had gone on to be a model and a celebrity depressive – though the word celebrity wasn't used liberally then. Afterwards, she had disappeared from view. Neil had given the photograph to the wrong person and had never made any money out of it. That had been the story, anyway.

Abe and Kirsty used to get palmed off on Neil two or three times a year because Gloria, their mother, thought he ought to be aware of them. When Gloria gave up accompanying them, the visits to Iverdale Road decreased and eventually stopped. Neil made no effort to keep in touch. On one occasion the children rang the bell and there was no reply. Abe climbed from the front steps on to the dirty windowsill to see, he said, if Neil was lying there dead. But he wasn't, so Abe and Kirsty went home. They often guessed information about him and got it wrong. Neil Rivers wasn't especially interested in children but he was brazen enough to get along with them – not supplicating. He had a husky voice that kept getting caught up on bits of itself, as if it were a frayed piece of rope, being pulled along a pipe. 'Hiya, kids,' he used to say when they walked in and, 'Fucking Ada,' in an up-and-down drawl, if things weren't going well. Having shown them where the biscuits were – in a tin with the pattern half missing – he left them alone. 'I'll take you out later,' he said. 'Think about where you want to go.' Then he sat at the kitchen table and opened the newspaper flat in front of him.

The first quarter of an hour visiting Neil at the house was always the worst. The children would stand still, getting used to the lack of attention. One part of them knew they had come to visit their father, but another part had no idea why they were there. They needed those minutes to think of him and get a grip. The bruised look to the parts of his face that he shaved, the shoulders hunched over the newspaper, the sticking-out backbones, like the beginnings of wings underneath his creased shirt, his height in relation to the ridged panes in the front door. He was tall; probably a fraction taller than Abe at man height, but it was hard to be accurate. Because Neil showed so little interest in them, Abe and Kirsty didn't believe that they would end up resembling him in any way. There was the haze of springy hair that all three of them had in common, though in different shades of brown – Abe's the colour of cassette tape, darker than his sister's. That had come from Grandad Abe. He was a GI who had had sex with Grandma Shirley and returned to America after the war. No one knew anything about him but judging by the Rivers hair and the even-toned skin that had no freckliness or pink to it he had been mixed-race. Kirsty had Gloria's grey-blue eyes. Girls' colour, Abe thought. Gloria had named her brown-eyed son after Grandad Abe because she thought he ought to be connected to his roots.

Abe used to tell Neil interesting facts about himself. Sports scores, swimming lengths, favourite football team, maths test results; he had them off pat. It suited him not to be interrupted or asked questions. He could keep going for about ten minutes. Kirsty had nothing to say. Having collected her biscuit she went back up to the hall. She stared up at the things that were out of reach: the box above the front door that contained the batteries for the doorbell; the dust-encrusted mouldings; the electric cable, fuzzy with dirt, from which the light bulb was suspended. Sometimes the telephone rang and then she ran, in panic, into the living room. The ringing stopped abruptly when Neil picked up the phone in the basement kitchen and Kirsty would hear him talking through the open door. She looked out of the window at the passing buses and the row of shops opposite, each decorated in different colours of chipped and faded paint but all kitted out with the same neon lighting. When she had had enough of that, she sat down self-consciously on the lumpy sofa and the assorted chairs, as if they were strangers' laps – pretending the strangers liked her. Draped over with faded Indian cloth, they seemed to her mostly female. Kirsty pressed her nose into the cushions and rugs and inhaled different flavours of dust, without being able to identify them. She wanted each to have a name as the battered enamel tins in the kitchen at home had names: coffee, tea, rice, bread. There were four floors to the house but, in essence, two halves separated by smell. Downstairs Kirsty could indulge her passion for sniffing. Upstairs, where Neil never ventured, the empty bedrooms and unused spare kitchen smelled uniform, cold and faintly vegetable, like dead cut flowers taken out of a vase. Kirsty used to go up there to breathe the difference and to examine the catches like windmills that fastened the cupboards. These things were enough. She went to visit Neil without complaining. Abe played on the stairs.

Going home to Crystal Palace on the train, Kirsty passed the time by practising Neil's intonation under her breath.

Abe, four years older, never joined in. He made a point of being himself – disavowing role models – though once or twice, at school, Kirsty thought she recognised Neil's slouch, as Abe sloped across the playground. 'What did you do at Neil's?' Gloria asked them.

'Played,' Abe said.

'Neil played with you?' Gloria said, with mock incredulity.

'Not really,' Abe answered.

'What did Kirsty do?'

'Nothing, as far as I know,' Abe said.

Gloria and Neil had been in love at the beginning but incompatible. Gloria was definite about that. She presented the love and the incompatibility as if they had both taken place on one eventful day. The real sequence of events – that, although failing to get on, she and Neil had had at least two mating periods of not being able to keep off each other – she skated over. Kirsty used to tell children at school that her parents were divorced. Abe didn't mention Neil at all past the age of eleven.

Neil Rivers died of liver cancer after only a few weeks in hospital. No one told his children, or the mother of his children, that he was ill, so they didn't go to see him. He was sixty. Abe's name was down on the hospital admissions form as Neil's next of kin, together with their old address and number. Gloria took the call informing them of the death and immediately rang her children. Abe was on the train, returning from Reading. Kirsty had just finished her finals. She was drinking with friends, on a triangle of green in front of a pub – lying on the grass with her possessions scattered around her: sunglasses, bags, flip-flops, phone.

Abe and Kirsty made arrangements to meet the next morning at St Mary's Hospital, Paddington. Then they went to the Register Office, which was in Wembley. They walked miles round the streets of west London because they kept going the wrong way. Kirsty was wearing strappy silver sandals that slipped whenever she stepped off a kerb. She wondered how people who were old or in an emotional state could cope. Abe, who was normally good with directions, wasn't concentrating. He was thinking of Neil answering the admittance questions at the hospital and saying 'Abe Rivers' when they asked who was next of kin. He kept stopping in the middle of the pavement and saying, 'He was our dad, Kirsty.' And in the end Kirsty told him to shut up because it was too late for any of that. They thought the solicitor was another formality. It never occurred to them that Neil had left them anything. They hadn't heard from him for years.

The solicitor said they could call her Colleen. She occupied a tiny room on a half-landing off a staircase, in premises above a shop. Her desk had black metal legs that looked like weaponry and clanged when you knocked a foot against them. The shelves round the walls were empty. Colleen said the building was being redecorated and that this wasn't her usual office. The three of them sat on plastic chairs; the type that stacked. Although the place lacked dignity, Kirsty wished she hadn't worn the short white sundress with the wavy hem. Abe looked grown-up and tidy in his work suit and pressed shirt. Colleen was encased in a tight jacket and skirt. She asked their ages – twenty-five and twenty-one – and checked their ID. There was no punctuation in the will Abe and Kirsty were given to look at, and they didn't understand at first that, between them, they owned a house. Neil himself had lived as if he were renting from a racketeer landlord. He had never shown any interest in his surroundings, nor in keeping them up. Colleen, who was also acting as Neil's executor, told them that Neil had left instructions that there should be no funeral, just the crematorium and nobody in attendance. She said she could recommend an undertaker, if they hadn't already chosen one. Abe and Kirsty didn't know what to say. They had never had to deal with death. Abe took his mobile out of his pocket and stared at it.

Colleen put on a different voice and told them that, unusually for London, even that part of London, the value of Neil's house probably fell below the inheritance tax threshold. Since their father had no other assets, with any luck they wouldn't need to pay anything to the Inland Revenue. Colleen assumed they would sell 105 Iverdale Road and turn it into nice crisp money. She smiled in a wincing kind of way as she described the poor state of repair of the house and its position on a main bus route. When she asked if Abe and Kirsty had any questions they were silent. They thanked her – they had had enough of her by then – and said they would be in touch. They went clattering down the stairs and across the road to a pub opposite and started on the beer. Abe rang up Gloria to tell her about the will, then passed the phone to Kirsty. 'Jammy bastards,' Gloria said. She had cried the previous evening when she heard that Neil was dead but she wasn't crying now. Kirsty asked her if it made her angry that Neil had never helped to pay for them or given them anything while he was alive. Gloria said no, she hadn't wanted his money. 'Knock and the door will have nothing behind it. Take what you can get, Sweets,' she said. 'Enjoy it.' After the day of dealing with weird official people, Abe and Kirsty felt suddenly elated, as if life had speeded up. They were giggly, almost hysterical. They kept clinking glasses, splashing the beer. 'If someone gave you a donkey or a camper van you would want to take it on at least one outing, wouldn't you?' Abe said. 'Give it a run around.' That summed up how they felt about the house. Abe said he would leave his job in Reading and take out a bank loan to do up his half of the property. He and Kirsty hugged each other and had more to drink, and the decision seemed irreversible.

In a lull Abe said, 'Is it all right, do you think, not doing anything?'

Kirsty went still. She knew what he was talking about. No funeral. Nothing. 'It's what he wanted,' she said. The sentence seemed the oddest thing she had ever said – more than grown-up, terrible. She wondered whether she might spend the rest of her life saying such things. She and Abe looked at each other.

Then Abe said 'I'm having upstairs' and everything was fine again. Kirsty remembered liking the downstairs; downstairs had more character. The top floors had always been peripheral.

After they left the pub, Abe went into town and Kirsty returned to the flat in New Cross that she shared with her boyfriend, Luka, and two second-year students, Zoë and Leanne.

Kirsty told Luka about Neil's house and said that she and Abe were going to move in together. Luka carried on pouring milk into his tea until the mug overflowed. Then, after a moment he said, 'But he's your brother.'

'And?' she said.

'You don't even like him.'

'Yes I do. He's been really helpful lately.'

Luka was letting the spilt tea drip over the edge of the table and just watching it.

It was true that Kirsty criticised Abe as a matter of routine. Some of the things he did left her breathless. Luka couldn't grasp that it's possible to feel more than one thing at a time, or even nothing at all plus one other feeling. It was natural to hate and love a brother. It felt quite normal. There was no need to agonise over it.

'We'll carry on seeing each other,' Kirsty said, stretching out to touch Luka's pale face. He looked very serious.

'*Will* we?' Luka jerked his head out of reach.

Kirsty hadn't asked him to move to Iverdale Road with her. The absence of the invitation hung there like a huge change of address card with only one name on it.

'This will be hard for Eugen,' Luka said. Eugen was his great friend – also from Croatia. He had had a short affair with Abe and turned gloomy when it ended.

'He'll get over it,' Kirsty said.

They stared at one another.

'You won't be on your own. Zoë and Leanne are still here,' Kirsty said.

'You didn't say you wanted to leave,' Luka said.

'This just happened, Luka. My dad died. I didn't plan it.'

'So you wouldn't have left in the foreseeable future?'

'I don't know,' Kirsty said. She remembered the cement-patched steps to Neil's front door and the gabled dormer window in the roof that looked like a silly miniature house in its own right. She had never heard Luka, or anyone young, talk about the foreseeable future. As a concept, it was impossible. He had probably been taught the phrase in English lessons at school in Zagreb.

Luka's eyes challenged her but Kirsty didn't rise. A picture – or a feeling – of a deep pot containing two children came to her. No one else, looking in, would know what it felt like down there. She felt the day – endless and exhausting – had been wasted. She and Abe should have taken everything more slowly. They shouldn't have laughed so much. Now the day was over and the only way to reclaim it would be to talk about the man who had been her father and to ask questions that had no answers. She wanted to understand how Neil could have ignored his children and then left them everything he possessed. She had said things in the wrong order and she couldn't go back. It was impossible to go back. If you changed one thing, everything changed.

4

Abe's feet shifted with the rhythm of the tube train. Warm air pumped through the ventilators inside the carriage and he took off his hat and scarf and stuffed them in his pockets. Deep in the underground tunnels weather was absent. The puny inch or so of snow that lay above ground was irrelevant, existing only as an anxious thought in the faces around him. Other passengers were standing but not so tightly packed that Abe was held steady by them. He ignored the overhead rail nearby – he didn't enjoy strap-hanging. He was aware of the need for balance and subtle footwork. Balance was a matter of the body – or was it of the mind? He could follow his thoughts, but only at a slight distance. Too close, and he lost the movement of the train and jolted sideways, as if coming to from a dream. Then he had to regain equilibrium. This took a few seconds.

Abe had woken with the beeping of an alarm clock. He had heard ticking though not from the clock. The ticks were loud, not quite regular – accompanied by gurgling from the other side of the room. He was baffled at first, then realised that he was in an unfamiliar room and the sounds were in the pipework. Water in a heating system was beginning to flow. Abe was aware of a strange posh smell that hung about the bedhead – new upholstery mixed with the kind of room spray that came in glass bottles. He opened an eye and saw the weird ruched curtains that trapped shadows in undulating lines. Richard was silhouetted against them, pulling on a bathrobe. Abe turned over into the place where Richard had been lying – warm as a jumper he had just taken off. He felt comfortable burrowed there but the next layer – beyond the hollow of the bed – he resisted. Abe stuck his nose back in the pillow. 'Is it still snowing?' he asked when he emerged.

'No, it seems to have stopped for the moment,' Richard said.

Abe was relieved. He wouldn't have wanted to be marooned at Richard's. He would have dug his way out.

They had taken showers in separate bathrooms. Richard had disappeared to the en suite and Abe had used the guest bathroom, decked out with an array of thick towels and baskets of miniature soaps and bath products. Abe picked them up and sniffed them. He made a face as he pulled the previous day's shirt over his head, missing the whiff of fabric conditioner, which, if he was on top of the washing, eased him into a new day.

Richard had made him breakfast – tea, cereal and toast. He turned on the kitchen television and they listened to the chirruping presenters. They heard the weather forecast and the travel news. The routine had gone smoothly, as if Abe were a regular house guest. As Abe was swallowing his last gulp of tea, Richard slipped his hand in his inside jacket pocket and muttered something about 'meeting up again'. A business card was pushed across the kitchen table. The action was commonplace enough but the words reminded Abe of his economics teacher who had said something similar on the last day of school. Abe had been polite and given Mr Owen a phone number. Realising that some similar response was called for, Abe patted his own pocket. Then, seeing the card with the feather on still lying where he had left it, he reached for it, took out a pen and scribbled a number down on the back – also out of politeness.

They had been ready to leave – Abe was putting on the

shoes that he had left by the front door – when the unhurried pace changed. Richard turned abruptly and shot back up the stairs that were tucked round the corner of the hall. Abe heard him above, walking across the bedrooms – checking up, Abe supposed. But he hadn't left anything – he had nothing to leave. The footsteps went to and fro. A cupboard door clicked. Abe thought of another kind of checking up. His bent head went hot, starting at the nape of his neck and moving over his skull to his forehead. Richard came back down again. From the corner of his eye, Abe saw that he had an odd, panicky look – but it wasn't suspicion. Abe could read suspicion on a face.

Richard stood fingering the buttons of his overcoat, as if wondering whether to undo them. 'You go on ahead,' he said to Abe, who was still crouching on the floor, tying his laces, tugging at them. Richard started to explain the way to the tube station.

'Cool,' Abe said about the explanation that had somehow taken the place of saying goodbye. Abe straightened up and left, shutting the door behind him. His last view was of Richard locked in position in the middle of the hall. It was as if the sight of a man doing up his shoes had unhinged him.

The trains out of Paddington Station were running sporadically. 'CANCELLED' appeared several times on the departures board and there was one deranged heading composed of a string of consonants. Among the positive entries was the Oxford service, which called at Reading. Abe bought a newspaper and a takeaway cup of coffee. There were no crowds; in fact, remarkably few people. Abe felt a change in mood – a lightening – as if he might be going on holiday. This buoyancy continued throughout the journey. The unusual brightness, reflected by the snow, shone through the dirty train windows. Once they left the built-up districts and were out in the open, Abe shifted across to a seat that was in shadow. He looked at the changed white fields. The countryside in the Thames Valley had expanded under the snow. He sipped at the coffee and enjoyed the scenery.

When Abe arrived at work he remained upbeat. Ben and Holly, who shared his office on the third floor of the slab-like building, had taken advantage of the transport chaos and called in, stranded. Liam, the boss, sent an e-mail round cancelling the weekly departmental meeting and kept his door, on the floor above, shut. This gave Abe a chance to progress BRAND BUILDING IN THE BUSINESS TO BUSINESS MARKET SECTOR but he failed to get started. The words sounded aggressive, reverberating round his head. Abe wandered about the empty spaces between the desks. He stared out at the similar premises across the courtyard; the figures inside, jackets discarded, sitting at their computers. If he moved his head to one side he could see some white in a gap between buildings. Usually it was green. That was Berkshire. Or maybe it was the university campus. He had never got to know Reading, only the walks to the station and to the pub round the corner.

Abe made a few calls not connected with work. He left a message for his friend Shane, suggesting they meet. Shane was hoping to start a business leasing Japanese exercise equipment to gyms and health clubs. He had asked Abe to go in with him. The equipment, Shane claimed, was superb. It made even the top-of-the-range stuff seem clunky. The machinery was powder-coated in soft colours and had some nice features, like the built-in screen that tracked the simulated run up Ben Nevis or the row along the Boat Race course between Putney and Hammersmith Bridges. Shane was planning to target spas and fitness centres. Abe hadn't said yes or no. He needed to check it out – but the idea of working for himself appealed to him. Maybe he'd go to Tokyo.

At lunchtime, Abe went down to the Beehive and ate a vegetarian chilli. It was on the Specials board. He returned to the office, feeling bloated from the chewy undercooked beans. The daylight was going. A dark patch of sky beyond the next building was spreading like dye across wet cloth. The fluorescent tubes that had glimmered redundantly throughout the morning now turned the office pink. Abe got down to work.

5

At six o'clock that evening Kirsty Rivers came out of a small shop tucked away behind Oxford Street on the north side. She set the burglar alarm, turned off the lights and pulled down the security shutter. There were no late nights at the shop – apart from the stocktake once a month – and no earlies either, whatever the weather. The business acted as an address, or an office, for people who didn't have one. Kirsty spent the day sending, receiving and forwarding mail. She wrapped up fragile and oddly shaped parcels. Gloria, her mother, couldn't understand why Kirsty was doing anything so lowly when she had a 2:1 in media and music. She said that if Kirsty was interested in post she should go and run the Post Office. It needed someone with a brain. Kirsty said that people of her age didn't run anything.

She was hungry so she crossed the road to the Lebanese grocer's opposite. A clear plastic sheet was draped over the display at the front and snow was collecting in the dips between the piles of fruit. Kirsty went inside and walked up one aisle and down the other, picking up a packet of halva, another of almonds and a bag of pleated cotton wool. The man behind the counter raised an eyebrow but Kirsty ignored it. She had decided, over time, that the eyebrow was not connected with the contents of the basket. The mind was elsewhere.

Leaving the smell of cold oranges, she walked along the backstreets towards Marble Arch. There was an enigmatic life behind Oxford Street that had nothing to do with department stores or tourist touts. Tall terraced houses were divided into offices. Drab lighting and the occasional chandelier shone behind full-length net curtains. There were black cars parked on yellow lines and occupied by sleek, sleeping drivers, newsagents selling foreign newspapers, tiny barbers' shops with only two chairs. Even in the snow, smartly dressed old women walked their dogs and waiters wrapped in tight white aprons sat on the back steps of hotels, sheltered by canopies. Kirsty liked the calm and the strangeness – the chink of unexplained money. She felt that however long she spent there she would lack information. She made her way to the Marble Arch end of Edgware Road and caught a bus. The lower deck was already crammed with people but the stream of incoming passengers continued boarding, squeezing into gaps fit only for flexible pipes. Kirsty forced her way up the stairs and stood on the upper deck, dipping into the nuts with her gloves on, munching them, lurching whenever the bus started and stopped. The windows were closed, steamy and running with water inside and out. Kirsty could feel the heat from the cough of the woman standing next to her. She tried to breathe shallowly. Her phone rang; it was Marlene.

'How was your New Year?' Marlene said.

'Don't ask,' Kirsty said.

'Tell me,' Marlene insisted in her compelling voice.

'Luka was working. He did an all-night stint at a bar, earning double time,' Kirsty said. 'He invited me along.'

'But you didn't go.'

'No.' Kirsty's conversations with Marlene generally reached a quick anticlimax. On the last stroke of midnight, Luka had rung to say the happy stuff. Kirsty had heard mayhem in the background – cheering and stamping and whooping singing. Abe had rung too at a quarter past twelve and shouted, 'Kirstabel, I love you. Why haven't you called to wish me Happy New Year?'

'*Something* happened,' Marlene said. 'I can hear you re-membering.'

'Two people said they loved me.' Kirsty glanced sideways at the woman with the cough.

'What were their names?' Marlene asked.

Kirsty paused. 'Luka and Abe.'

Marlene sighed.

'I made a cup of tea and took it to bed but I fell asleep before I'd drunk it,' Kirsty said.

'It can only get better, Kirst. I hate that new beginning propaganda. It's not real. Since when was January a new beginning? I read your stars for the year and it said, "You already have wings. Soon you will fly."' Then Marlene said that she had a call waiting and rang off.

Kirsty put the phone in her pocket and took out the almonds again.

'You'll never get fat,' the woman with the cough said. 'However many nuts you eat.'

After almost an hour, the bus reached Kensal Rise. Kirsty began to ease her way down, edging past the people who were standing on the stairs. By the time she was at the bottom, the bus was at the Iverdale Road stop. Kirsty stepped off and skidded across the pavement in her shoes with wafer-thin soles. She never planned ahead with shoes, perhaps because the house was only twenty metres from the stop – a mixed-brick terraced house with a scruffy hedge at the front. Some terraces have a look of uprightness but this one needed shared walls to prop itself up. The roof sprouted buddleia – charred-looking spikes that resisted the snow. Kirsty's footsteps were the first since the snowfall, though the slush thrown up by the traffic spattered the front path. No one had walked up to deliver pizza flyers and Abe wasn't yet back. He hadn't come home the previous night. Sometimes he stopped out for days at a time. Kirsty placed her feet gingerly on the ice-covered steps and opened the door. The house, punctured by gaps in the woodwork, felt as cold as a shed. Apart from the rumble of buses outside, the place was quiet. No sound of Abe's builders from the upper floors, though they often worked in the evenings.

Kirsty went down to the basement, still with her coat on, holding the roll of cotton wool. She pulled pieces off and stuffed them into the joins of the warped window frames where shafts of air were coming in. She felt as if she were tending wounds, patching up lesions, but then, when she finished, the windows looked like a home for cocooned butterflies. The draught was tamed. On a whim, Kirsty switched off the lights. She skirted round her bed in the dark and went back to the window to look at the garden refashioned by snow. She tried to guess what lay beneath; the bumps and stumps that had once been a bucket, a deckchair frame, a wheel from a motorbike. It felt odd to be staring from the unlit house – a quirky thing that she would never have done in ordinary weather. The buildings in the next street seemed suddenly much closer and more companionable, as if they were part of a village – not a picturesque village, but a place where, once upon a time, you might have spoken to your neighbours. She stayed for about ten minutes, just staring out.

When Abe returned at eight o'clock, Kirsty was preparing her supper – chopping up garlic and onions to cook with some rice and chickpeas.

'Nothing fucking works in this country,' he said, as he walked into her kitchen. Abe generally came in to see her, if he had nothing better to do. He sounded cheerful. He waved the evening paper and slapped it down next to her on the speckled Formica worktop, like a husband in a fifties film. Kirsty glanced at the fuzzy picture of lines of cars, stranded in white drifts on a motorway. She moved the newspaper to one side because it was half over the chopping board, on top of the bits of garlic.

'Let's have a party at the weekend,' Abe said, putting an

arm round her and picking a chickpea out of the open tin with his free hand. 'A house-warming.'

'You've had one already,' Kirsty said, extricating herself from the cold sleeve.

'Oh, *that* wasn't a proper party,' Abe said. 'That was just having a few friends round. We'll have a proper one and you come to it this time. We'll use the whole house.'

Abe had celebrated every major purchase he had made: the American-style fridge, the high-speed shower, the wide-screen television. On these occasions he drank a lot of Prosecco and took various drugs.

'I won't know anyone,' Kirsty said.

'Of course you will. Ask people.'

'Will Declan be coming?'

'No idea,' Abe said.

Declan was a musician who played recorder and flute. Kirsty had known him at university. He alternated between animation and Zen-like calm, and had furrows running from his nose to his chin that made him look older than he was. He and Abe had got it on – at least Kirsty assumed so because at one time she kept bumping into him around the house. She hadn't seen him since before Christmas but he had left his bicycle, a black waterproof and a stack of CDs in the hall. It was funny thinking of the people – men – who started out as her friends and then fancied her brother. They tended to drift away after an involvement with Abe. She had lost a few friends that way. Kirsty ran a knife down the papery casing of an onion and began peeling it, section by section. From the corner of her eye, she saw Abe pull off his hat and stuff it into his coat pocket. Then he took off the coat and draped it over a chair.

'Do you want to know what happened to me yesterday?' he said.

'Go on.'

'First, I had to fight my way off the train.' Abe paused. He roamed around the room. He opened one of the kitchen cupboards and shut it again. He opened another and started moving things about.

'What are you doing, Abe?'

'I thought you might have some raisins.'

'I haven't.'

He carried on poking around inside.

'What are you looking for now?'

'Nothing.' He pulled out a small packet. 'Why have you got an elastic band round these walnuts?'

'To stop them falling out.'

'Neat.' He was already chewing. 'They're a bit stale.' Abe dipped into the packet again. 'Anyway, like I said, eventually, I got through to the taxi queue outside Paddington Station. What?' he asked, interrupting himself, catching some expression on Kirsty's face.

'I didn't say anything. Carry on.' Kirsty blinked as the vapour came off the onion and a dribble of juice ran out.

'You never take black cabs. I know.' Abe leant his head back and tipped the remaining particles of walnuts into his mouth. Then he continued. He didn't name the man he had shared the taxi with, or say anything about him, other than that he lived in Sudbury Hill. He described the journey in detail, making it sound like the snow scene in *Narnia*. Kirsty carried on chopping the onion, rhythmically slicing it into smaller and smaller pieces. Abe reached the point where the man offered to put him up for the night. He stopped. Kirsty put down the knife and looked up at him. The story had come to an end. She hadn't said anything; she had just let him tell it. Abe was smiling. It was his silly lips-together smile that went on for hours. Kirsty couldn't see what he was so pleased about.

'You told this man you lived in *Harrow*?' Kirsty said. 'You've never even been there, have you?'

'No,' Abe agreed. 'Why would I want to go to Harrow?'

'What did this man look like, then?' Kirsty asked.

'Gorgeous,' Abe said.

'Gorgeous?'

'Yeah. Why not?' Abe started to laugh.

'What's he called?'

'Richard.'

'He doesn't have another name?'

'Could be Epworth.'

'Are you seeing him again?'

'I wouldn't have thought so. Is there a bottle open?'

'No.'

Abe opened the fridge and closed it again. 'Have you got *anything* to drink?'

'Just water.'

Abe looked sceptical but he picked up his coat. 'See you.'

6

On Saturday night, Kirsty heard the front door slam and the uneven pulse of feet tramping upstairs to Abe's party. She retreated to her bathroom in the basement and immersed herself in hot water. Voices and music from Abe's rooms – occasional shouts of laughter – were relayed down the pipework and distorted by strange echoes. By the time she got out of the bath the house was throbbing. Kirsty went into her bedroom and shut the door. The smell of dope seeped under it. Kirsty lay in bed with the duvet pulled over her head. She was conscious of pressure on the framework of the house but she slept. Halfway through the night people started to leave. Then she woke up. Minicab drivers hooted in the street or pounded up the steps and rang the doorbell. The tramping happened in reverse. Once, someone fell down the stairs. Once, someone knocked over Declan's bicycle, making it clatter on the hall floor.

At about two o'clock on Sunday afternoon Luka came round.

'What's all this?' he asked, pointing at the bin liners piled by the front path and crammed full of bottles and cans. The smell of stale alcohol hung around like old smoke.

'It's Abe's rubbish. He had a party,' Kirsty said. 'The bin men don't come till Tuesday.'

'Did you go to the party?' Luka looked bedraggled in his wet jeans and fleece. The snow had turned to rain overnight, and his hair was as flat to his head as a black bathing cap.

'No,' Kirsty replied.

'Place stinks,' he said, as he walked through the front door, carrying a plastic bag containing chicken curry from the Caribbean café along Iverdale Road.

'Thanks.'

He generally brought food with him – sometimes take-aways, sometimes minced beef or sausages from the super-market, which Kirsty would cook. He was fixed up with various evening jobs – shelf filling, bar work, shop security – menial employment for a graduate of the University of Zagreb but the only type of employment available if you had 'NO WORK OR RECOURSE TO PUBLIC FUNDS' stamped in your passport. Sunday afternoon was one of the few times he and Kirsty were both free. He came alone. Eugen refused to visit the Iverdale Road house in case he met Abe. It still felt strange not seeing Eugen – someone vaguely in the way of their relationship. They had grown accustomed to his being there. Kirsty and Luka ate the food and watched DVDs and had sex, all on her bed. In the New Cross flat they had lived in one room and Luka seemed to want to carry on that way. It was dark by about four o'clock, so they drew the curtains and put the lights on, and it felt later than it was.

'See you next week, Kirsty,' Luka said when it was time to go. Then he left and the evening was still free. Kirsty felt less committed somehow than if he had stayed the night. She didn't feel inwardly committed. She cleared away the takeaway cartons and the wafers of Rizla paper that fell out of Luka's pockets. She went up to the living room, picked up her guitar and played a few chords. Fragments of words and music came to her, clear but evanescent. They came and went. There was a flavour to a song, at the back of her mind – serene and burnt at the edges, like a good day that carries on too long – but she couldn't give it life.

She tried singing random words that might fit but she

sounded fake to herself and gave up. She listened to the hum of the traffic and looked at the gap where the curtains failed to meet, watching the brightness rush in whenever a bus went past. Somehow, her creative mood failed to coincide with the times she was free. As a student, she had sung in pubs and clubs but she had nothing to show for the last few months. Her only musical activity had been to sort out the CDs that Declan had left in the hall. Even that hadn't gone as planned. Abe had asked her what they were and she had said, 'What do you mean, what are they? They're all different.'

And he'd said, 'Well, they weren't all written in the same year, were they? What order do they go in? I don't know anything about that sort of music.' So although the collection was pretty eclectic, Kirsty had started him on Gregorian chant and sorted the rest into chronological order as best she could. For a time, Pachelbel and Albinoni had resounded through the house, then, 'I'm going to have to skip this next bit,' Abe had said, some time around the eighteenth century, 'I can't handle it.' It was like the games they used to play. Abe always backed out halfway through.

Kirsty went into the hall. She put on the coat that was hanging over the post at the foot of the stairs and left the house. Sunday travel was slow – a bit of a mission – but Kirsty caught a bus to Victoria and waited on the station for a train to Crystal Palace, retracing the old route home. She felt more impatient with herself than with the journey. As the train crossed the Thames, she looked through the window at the twinkling lamps of Chelsea Bridge, elongated into frayed strands of light by the sleet. The four towers of Battersea power station loomed above the tracks. Kirsty took off the scarf that Luka had given her for Christmas. It was woolly on one side and velvety on the other with stitching to keep the two sides together. Lying coiled in her lap, it seemed like a sleeping animal. She stroked it absent-mindedly. She realised how tired she was, but it wasn't physical tiredness. She thought of the Sunday afternoons she and Luka had spent since she moved to Iverdale Road; the same pattern every time – food, DVD, sex – in her basement bedroom. The first of these afternoons had been just like the others, only it was the first. Luka was mostly irritable; though that didn't stop him wanting to make love to her or keep hold of her as he dropped off to sleep. She was like a favourite doll, taking up little room in the bed. He clung to her and she responded to his touch.

At Crystal Palace Kirsty got off the train. There were still traces of snow at the far end of the platform. Kirsty took a gulp of south London air and pulled her phone out of her pocket. The rectangle of light glowed in the dark. She stared at it for a moment but she didn't call Gloria. She thought of the walk from the station and the chance of an empty house. Gloria was often out. She crossed over to the up platform and travelled back to Victoria, past the dark tracts of common streaked with snow and the streets that showed their reverse side to the rail track. She felt different from when she had set out. She had put in the miles. Some part of her mind was loosened.

At the beginning of February, when the sky seemed higher, Kirsty got round to painting the kitchen walls and cleaning out the insides of cupboards. She had always thought that the transition from girl to adult meant having more of life on the outside – both material things in place but also shifting the balance from pretending to doing – less daydreaming. The new ice-blue paint was thick and creamy, with an intensity that didn't last once the brush went in, and wasn't recreated on the uneven surface. Kirsty didn't mind that the look wasn't perfect. Living among the remnants of Neil's things, she felt sheltered from the builders banging and drilling above her. Abe hadn't hung on to anything. He had hired a skip and everything had gone into it: the beige mottled lino and the squares of patterned carpet with their edges bound in tape, the green-streaked bath, the kitchen units made of Formica.

There hadn't been so much up there but it looked a lot in the skip.

Kirsty went to the local hardware shop and bought some checked zip-up bags that opened out like boxes. It seemed the right moment to clear out all the remaining stuff that was in Luka's flat. Summer clothes, unwearable clothes, binders full of notes and coursework. Kirsty took the bags to New Cross. The flat smelled of shower gel and burnt toast. Zoë and Leanne were both in the kitchen. They were wearing suede boots with high heels and straightening their already flat English hair with hair straighteners. They hugged Kirsty and offered her coffee. Kirsty felt that a gulf existed between them. She remembered being a student but as if it were a faraway time she had left behind.

Kirsty crossed the landing and went into Luka's room. An enlarged version of a photo that Luka had taken of her the previous summer was stuck on the wall and a strip of different, passport-size photos of her was wedged into a corner of the mirror. Otherwise nothing had changed. The row of empty Croatian beer bottles was still lined up on the radiator. Kirsty walked to the window and stared out over the railway tracks. The first train that went by set the whole room juddering and then, a few minutes later, two passed each other and let off piercing screeches. Kirsty took her clothes out of the cupboard, then redistributed Luka's jeans and T-shirts evenly along the hanging rail to close the gap. Opening and shutting drawers in a haphazard fashion, she came across jokey things Luka had given her: badges, worry beads, a yo-yo, a plastic cactus. She hesitated, wondering whether to take them or leave them. In the end, she added them to her collection. There was too much to carry, so she left one of the bags behind in the room. She called out goodbye to Zoë and Leanne. It took about an hour and a half to reach Iverdale Road on public transport. Having dumped the bags, she went back to New Cross. Luka and Eugen were there the second time, sitting on the floor, watching sport on television. At least they weren't on the bed. She told Luka that she was clearing her stuff out. He nodded without taking his eyes from the screen. It felt odd to be ignored when there were pictures of Kirsty Rivers stuck around the room.

When Luka came over on the following Sunday, Kirsty told him she wanted to stop the afternoons and said she hoped they could be friends. Luka wanted to know why and she said the afternoons were a bit monotonous and that she needed a break. He said everything would be different once he got a day job. His evenings and nights would be free. She said that wasn't what she meant. They were lying on the bed but she got up then and started to put her clothes on. He pressed and pressed her, and she had to say she wasn't in love with him, which didn't sound nice spoken out loud. She couldn't see why she had to say it after only fourteen months, or however long it was that they'd been together. He got up and sat on the edge of the bed. He said, 'Come here, Kirsty,' and she had to let him hold her, which didn't work with him sitting and her standing. She ended up sitting on his knee. He was naked and she had some of her clothes on, and it was all ridiculous.

Two

1

Vivienne Epworth looked out of the window of Starbucks.

'It's had quite a history, that china cabinet,' her mother was saying. 'We found it in ...'

'Westmoreland,' Vivienne said.

'Yes, darling, exactly. When Westmoreland *was* Westmoreland. I shall never know why they gave up those lovely county names. In a village, I can't remember where precisely. Though we had just crossed the border from Cumberland. We were travelling around. We used to do that a lot before you were born. Such a camp little man in the shop. It was a bookshop but he also sold antiques. There was some jewellery on a willow-pattern dish. I tried on a brooch, little garnets in a crescent shape, and he said, "Be careful, dear, the pin is rather *acute*." Daddy and I often laughed about that.'

Vivienne and her mother, Frances, were in Beaconsfield, which was close to where Frances lived. The cabinet referred to was several miles away in the corner of Frances's dining room, with an old print of Alnwick Castle to its left and a pencil sketch of two little girls, Frances and her sister, Jane, to the right. Frances could summon up pieces of her furniture like genies from a bottle. The rain hadn't left off; it spotted the glass and stained the road dark. A charity sales tout, a tall ponytailed girl wearing a green tunic, was hailing passers-by. She was especially physical – extending her arms and barricading the way. People walked round her, raising their umbrellas, stepping off the kerb to give her a wide berth. Even the elderly, of whom there were many in Beaconsfield, laboriously manoeuvred their shopping trolleys off and then on again, as if the girl were a burst water main or a piece of street furniture, maybe a bollard. Frances was facing inwards with her back to the street. She adored Starbucks. She liked the sofas and the newspapers and the froth in the coffee. She said the name as if it fizzed. There was no persuading her. To her it seemed young and louche and, compared with the place some of Frances's friends went to, which had pink paper napkins and served coloured hot water, Vivienne acknowledged that she had a point.

Vivienne had been seeing her mother for Lent. Every Friday morning. Her daughters, Bethany and Martha, had given up chocolate. Richard had given up alcohol and she, Vivienne, had given up her free morning. For the rest of the week she worked at a bathroom design centre in Ruislip where she was manager. Friday was the only time that felt approximately her own. The self-denial wasn't pure mortification; it had a weary purpose behind it. Perhaps this was always the case with mortification. Vivienne needed to steel herself for the task and Easter was a convenient deadline.

For nearly a year Frances had talked of downsizing – trading in her ample semi, with its stairs and landings, for neater accommodation all on one level. She had lived alone since her husband, Vivienne's father, died, coping for most of that time, though routine turned into effort. Frances wished her house would shrink. 'I need an easy-to-manage box,' she said. 'Preferably above ground. I'm going to be seventy, you know. Three score years and ten. That's Your Chap's recommended cut-off point.' She had accumulated piles of particulars but refused to visit prospective properties on her own – by which she meant without Vivienne – citing random hazards such as wet floors, marble floors, unexpected changes of level involving steps, vendors who didn't speak up, vendors who weren't her sort of people.

They had clocked up three of these mornings already. This was the fourth. They followed a pattern: viewings, then coffee and, over coffee, Frances verbally arranged her furniture around the properties viewed and failed to fit it in. Vivienne could see the arrangement going on for ever. House-hunting involved so many things that gave Frances pleasure: talking to strangers, looking at people's possessions, being driven round half-remembered suburban lanes, having her daughter to herself. She hadn't been told that she was a Lenten penance. The weekliness had been a mistake, Vivienne reflected, wondering whether she should have factored in a lapse. Was it even possible to factor in a lapse? The slippery nature of the word suggested not. Richard, for instance, would undoubtedly have benefited from a relaxing glass of wine. He had been rather low since New Year and uninterested in sex, even on an occasional basis. Once or twice when he was working on an audit away from London she had the silly idea that the change of scene might ginger him up. Rather self-consciously, on the night of his return – or on edge the following morning because of the girls and the time factor – she waited for Richard to make a move and he didn't. So she didn't.

Vivienne tucked her sleek short hair behind her ears and touched one of her moonstone earrings, twisting it round in the piercing. Perhaps the absence was never long enough. She stared out at the rain.

The previous evening, Prayer Clinic had prayed for a couple called Ross and Julia. Ross had been diagnosed as having a rare cancer but had failed to tell Julia. He had even *had treatment* without telling her. Julia was a friend of one of the group – not herself a member of St Dunstan's – so, in the general chat afterwards, they had discussed the situation in some detail. Prayer Clinic was in some ways rather like Book Club, where everyone ended up talking about characters and their actions in relation to their own lives, only in Prayer Clinic the comments were more respectful and sympathetic because the people were real. Everyone present, including Vivienne, had agreed it was impossible that any of their husbands would have withheld information about a serious illness, or that they themselves wouldn't have known intuitively that something was wrong. She hadn't been quite truthful. Even as she heard herself chiming in, saying the same as the others, only in a slightly different way, she could imagine all too clearly Richard keeping quiet – being brave and hoping to be cured without fuss. She should have said, 'Hang on a minute. I made a mistake. Richard might well be a Ross-type person. He's very uncommunicative.' Her proclaimed confidence in female intuition had also been wishful thinking. Her own was almost certainly faulty, like a lamp with a poor connection.

Vivienne's friend, Paula de Witt, would have shone a light into the dimmest corners of Hartley, her husband. Everything about Paula was on full power. She was even able to witness – had the nerve to witness – stopping people in the street and talking to them about their insecurities and inviting them to groups and Sunday worship at St Dunstan's. She had a super smile and thick fair hair, which she secured with bright-coloured combs. Vivienne was only able to hand out leaflets. That was hazardous enough, since people were often quite rude. She recalled the man, wearing a Stetson, standing on the traffic island at Piccadilly Circus, addressing the crowds with the help of a microphone. She had examined his expression – the blank look in his eyes – and wondered if it was panic.

'Where shall we go next week, darling?' Frances was asking. 'I'm tempted by Princes Risborough, or do you think that's too far out? You're the one who would have to make the journey. In an emergency it would be a long way for you to drive.'

'What sort of emergency?' Vivienne picked up her cup of coffee and drained it. Some aspect of the depressing street scene – or her mother's voice – had influenced her mood. She was shocked that Frances had abandoned fitting her furniture into the flats they had visited that morning. She had only got halfway through the second property that they had looked around. She hadn't reached the most promising one yet: a pleasant flat in Burnham Beeches with a lift and a wide balcony, large enough to sit out on. She *was* in it just for the ride.

Frances looked wistful. 'If anything should happen to me.'

'Something's far more likely to happen to you in "Lostwithiel" at the far end of the garden or coming down the front steps. You know how steep they are. They also have that odd dip in the middle where the frost settles,' Vivienne said.

'Please don't use that horrible word, dear. The house has a number, not a name.'

'It's engraved on the wall.'

'Well, we never look at it and it's not part of the address,' Frances said. 'Nobody uses it.'

Vivienne reached down for her bag and took out her purse. It gave her a jolt when her mother said 'we' in the present tense, as if her father's death had been a trick and Frances actually had him banged up in a cupboard. She had always organised Douglas, and his death hadn't put an end to that. 'She's out of the house. Now's your chance, Daddy,' Vivienne muttered. She hoped he had had some quiet moments of rebellion.

'What was that?' Frances asked.

Vivienne shook her head. Somewhere she had jotted down what time the pay and display ticket ran out. The array of cards in her purse, debit and credit, the loyalty store cards, the wodge of banknotes, suggested she was grown-up. 'I really think the best thing would be for you to go through all the particulars we've collected so far and decide which of the flats you'd like to see a second time,' she said. 'The agents will stop taking you seriously if you keep flitting from place to place. And you should put the house on the market. It's the right time of year.'

'Flitting, did you say? Surely not, darling.'

'They'll lose interest,' Vivienne said. 'They want to tie up deals.'

Frances shuddered slightly. 'So, you're saying no to Princes Risborough?'

'I am,' Vivienne agreed. 'Are you ready to go, Mummy? There aren't many minutes left.'

The chugger with the ponytail and green tunic had stopped someone. A man with tinted spectacles and a white stick. How insensitive of the girl to have collared someone too blind to avoid her. Vivienne was shocked. She hoped he wouldn't agree to anything.

'We need to pay, darling. I think it's my turn, isn't it?' Frances said in her sweetest voice.

'I paid at the counter when we came in,' Vivienne said. 'We're in Starbucks.'

2

Parking near the de Witts' for their annual Easter lunch was a problem – made worse since a couple of innocuous cafés at the end of the road had been smartened up and now attracted late breakfasters who sat around in cashmere scarves. The streets and cul-de-sacs of stuccoed Victorian houses were lined with cars. One or two of Paula and Hartley's guests double parked, hoping the locals would be lenient in this well-decorated part of west London, but Richard Epworth considered the strategy risky. A scratch etched along the side of the car, or an outraged note, would ruin his day. He found a spot nearly a quarter of a mile away and he and the family walked briskly. A cold wind drove them along the pavement. Easter was early.

A smiling young woman from a catering company opened the front door and directed people down to the open-plan basement. Another stood at the foot of the stairs, with a tray of glasses filled with sparkling wine or fresh orange juice. Talk was loud, trapped under the low ceiling, but Paula's greetings rose above it. Richard edged his way down the stripped-pine stairs, hampered by children who pushed past his legs. Arriving at the tray, he chose the wine – his first drink since the start of Lent. He grasped the glass by its stem and made for a patch of empty space. There was already quite a crowd; familiar-looking adults, fresh from church, wearing confident colours. Paula had filled the room with flowers – white tulips and Madonna lilies. 'Where's the bride?' someone boomed. Richard took a large sip from the glass.

'Vivienne and the girls here?' The face, close to Richard's, which appeared to conceal two symmetrically placed boiled sweets in the lower jaw, was topped by a fuzz of greyish hair. Everything below the face was dominated by a yellow V-necked jersey, stretched over a prominent stomach. A pair of beige trousers was belted beneath the curve.

'Somewhere,' Richard said. 'I lost them at the top of the stairs.'

'Any plans for the holiday?'

'No. I go back to work on Tuesday. How about you?' Richard took another gulp. He didn't recognise the man though the fellow seemed to know who he was.

'Off to France this evening to check up on the builder. See if he's managed to saw through any more pipes,' the man said.

'Sounds fun.'

'Three times he's done it. Numero uno, *notre ami* went through the mains – massive great fountain, high as the trees – cut off the neighbours' water supply. Madame et Monsieur were none too pleased, I can tell you, started jabbering on about *indemnité*. They seemed to care more about that than getting the damned thing mended ... '

The man was in full flood, looking over Richard's shoulder, somewhere past his left ear. The oblique gaze made Richard feel paranoid and slightly woozy, as if the room had tipped. The ceiling seemed oppressively near his head. He closed his eyes and took a few deep breaths.

'Is something the matter, my friend?' The man was holding Richard's elbow and looking at him with concern. The jersey was brighter than previously. God, it was bright.

'No, no,' Richard said, releasing himself. 'I'm absolutely fine. Just forgot where I was for a moment. Nothing to worry about.'

Vivienne appeared at Richard's side. 'Vivienne, my dear.

You're looking neat.' The man took her hands and held her at arm's length, before kissing her. 'Hang on. *A la française*, please. That's at least three times in our village.' He kissed her twice more, making more luscious contact each time. Vivienne waited, smiling faintly. Her right cheek glistened. 'I was just about to say to Richard it could be petit mal, this lapse thing,' the man said. 'Go and see a good neurologist. I can recommend someone if you like. Get him checked out.'

Vivienne looked puzzled. Richard raised his eyebrows a couple of times at her in what he hoped was a comic French manner.

'How's the bespoke bathroom business?' the man asked Vivienne.

Richard took the opportunity to slip away. He dodged between a woman in a delphinium-blue jacket and Glen, the vicar of St Dunstan's, who touched his forehead in a mock salute as Richard passed. One of the patio doors on to the garden was propped open and although the draught coming through the gap was chilly and a dozen children, including his own, were racing round the lawn, Richard stepped outside.

'Darling. Happy Easter,' Paula said. 'You look as if you could do with a top-up. If Poppy doesn't appear with the bottle, I'll go and get you one myself as soon as I've blown the starting whistle for the Easter egg hunt. Do you want to blow the whistle? You could, you know.'

'No, I'm sure you'll do it better than me. Super party,' Richard said. He was glad to be in the fresh air.

Paula pushed back the fair curls that were lifting in the wind. She was wearing a red wind-proof coat over her party dress and had a whistle on a ribbon round her neck. 'Just look at the energy these guys have,' she said.

Under the flowering fruit trees the children were gathering up handfuls of wind-blown blossom and chasing each other, flinging petals that never met their targets. They were hopeless projectiles. The little ones kept on trying, hurling with greater and greater force, but Bethany, Richard's elder daughter, and an older boy whom Richard didn't recognise, changed tactic. They began closing in on the children, grabbing whoever they could get hold of and cramming petals down their necks. Martha, his younger daughter, wasn't taking part. She was at the far end of the garden by the summer house. Enveloped in Vivienne's pashmina, she stood on one leg and clasped the foot of her raised leg behind her. She hopped on the spot, staring at her reflection in the glass doors of the summer house, hopping closer and closer, until the pashmina slid off her head and on to the floor. Then, wearing only her vest and knickers, she stood with her bare feet digging into the cloth, and began to twirl round and round until the folds had wound in a spiral up to her ankles. She was more fragile-looking than her sister – more Vivienne's build – with the same pale skin like the inside of shells. Richard wondered where her clothes had gone. He called her name but she ignored him.

'I am counting to ten.' It was Bethany's voice above the squealing. 'Starting from now. One. Two. Three. Four ... '

The squeals changed to shrill screams. One little girl was already down on the ground with the older boy lying on top of her, apparently strangling her. Another had crashed into a tree, trying to escape, and was sobbing.

'Probably time for chocolate,' Paula said. She put the whistle to her lips and gave a long blast. 'Right, guys. Easter egg hunt. All stand up. When I blow the whistle again, all you little kids start hunting for eggs round the patio. Try not to hurt the daffodils. Conrad and Bethany, there are two *special* eggs in the front garden. Go and wait by the side gate. I'll let you through in a minute.'

'Brilliant,' Richard said. He took out his handkerchief and wiped his face. The wine was making him sweat.

The children were all on their feet. Conrad, flushed and

panting, looked as though he regretted abandoning the fleshly sin of strangling for the uncertain promise of egg collecting. The child who had banged her nose stopped crying. Martha, at the far end of the garden, bent down and untangled her feet from the pashmina. She picked it up and wrapped it round her head, flipping the ends behind her with an elegant flourish. She sped across the garden, as if energised by the confinement of her head – the concealment of her hair – and disappeared indoors. Paula blew the whistle again. The young children ran towards the house and started to scrabble in the pots and raised beds. Bethany walked past Paula and Richard towards the gate in a self-important way. She didn't acknowledge her father. 'Hurry up, Conrad,' she called over her shoulder.

'Darling.' Paula turned to Richard. 'Be an angel and keep an eye on the tiddlers while I go through to the front. There should be three eggies each. Something like that.' She put her hand into her coat pocket and, having pulled it out again, grasped Richard's hand and filled it with foil-wrapped eggs. 'Make sure no one gets left out,' she said, moving away.

'*Are* there special ones in the front garden,' Richard asked.

'Any minute now there will be,' Paula replied. 'Richard, you are such a *boy*.'

Was he? Vivienne often looked at him as if she discerned arrested development and he didn't necessarily disagree with that. He had a core that had remained the same since he was, say, eight or nine, possibly younger. Yet he knew from observing children, his own and other people's, that he was no longer the same person. He was hurt and pleased, as the children were – as he had once been – and those feelings of hurt and pleasure tapped straight into parts of him that were like old underground watercourses. But the rise and fall of his moods was different. Flatter, certainly, if they could be plotted – shot through by surprise but not by outrage. He sometimes wondered if his children were genuinely outraged.

Their reaction was so extreme. They relished outrage for its own sake, putting on astonished faces and, in Bethany's case, more often than not, planting her hands on her hips as if she were about to begin line dancing.

Richard, nursing his empty glass, glanced back at the house to see if Poppy was in evidence. Having started on the wine he didn't want to stop. The numbing effect was welcome. He saw through the window that Vivienne was still trapped by Petit Mal. She seemed younger than the other adults, a slight figure in a simple sweater dress, with the look of a girl who has borrowed her mother's high-heeled shoes. Petit Mal towered over her. Richard recognised her expression; the well-mannered passivity. She was too polite to move away and talk to someone else, but he could tell that she wasn't actually listening. Getting around at parties was a skill. He wasn't sure he had acquired it. Naturally, no one expected you to stay talking to them until a substitute turned up, but sometimes at these gatherings he felt as if he were simply standing to attention and longing for the Changing of the Guard. He tended to stick it for as long as he could and then bolt.

One of the catering girls had wriggled through the crowd and was proffering an oversized tray. Petit Mal was picking up a little mound and holding it as if he thought it might fall apart. He was conveying the morsel towards Vivienne's mouth, which opened into a reluctant O. Richard turned back towards the garden, glad to have been given a task that allowed him to be unsociable. Easter was a funny time of year. The March sky was grey as an old sheet, behind the extravaganza of blossoms – flower on flower bursting from wood. Who could have thought of that combination? It was a way of throwing nature into maximum relief; an excess of excess which he didn't know what to do with – perhaps no one knew. The children didn't look up into the branches. They were happy, picking off bits of coloured foil from the eggs they had found and placidly munching chocolate.

*

'You're young. Perhaps you can answer this question,' Richard said when Poppy stepped outside and came towards him with the bottle.

'I'll try,' Poppy said brightly. Her face was nursery-fresh, at odds with her height and the breasts, under the thin white shirt, that were straining against the cloth and an inner layer of white lace.

'It's about music,' he said.

'OK.' Poppy refilled his glass.

'Have you heard of *Ba-roque*?' Richard asked, leaving a hint of a pause between the two syllables with a degree of self-consciousness.

'Yes, of course,' Poppy answered.

'Would I like them? Give me an album name.'

'Vivaldi?' she suggested. '*The Four Seasons*?'

'Really? Nothing more recent? Are you sure?' Richard tried to catch hold of her arm but she disappeared with her bottle and napkin, through the patio doors and into the crowd, her ponytail swinging as she went. Richard followed.

He was hoping for food, but before he reached the table he was importuned by the woman in the delphinium-blue jacket. 'You're Richard, aren't you?' she said, planting a foot in front of his. He nodded. 'I'm Isobel – but everyone calls me Bellsie.' Her earrings jangled like wind chimes as she moved her head. 'What stage are your girls at?' she asked.

'Early,' Richard said.

The woman laughed. 'You've obviously been asked the question several times already.'

'Some of the time they're grown-up.'

'And do they get *on*?' she asked, emphasising the last word as if it were something significant.

'Bethany's quite bossy but otherwise, yes.' Richard felt extraordinarily tired.

'A phase, I expect. My Hugh is thirteen. He's in a curious one at the moment.'

Richard waited but Bellsie didn't elaborate. 'My father has a theory about phases,' he said. 'Says that it's important not to get stuck in them. Keep moving on. For instance, if you're wondering whether to marry, change jobs, have a child – do the thing, get on with it. Life's all in the future.' He was aware that he had attempted too many sentences at a stretch. His speech was blurring. Or was it his thoughts? Father, with his thumbs tucked into the belt loops of his grey flannel trousers, would have been more assured.

'He sounds rather unusual,' Bellsie said. 'Alternative.'

'No. No, he isn't. A very ordinary, mild-mannered man. The phase he got stuck in began when he was about twenty-eight. There's been nothing new since then. Nothing.'

'Oh de-ar,' Bellsie said.

Robbie Patterson sang a creamy tenor. And Jennifer Patterson played the piano. Jennifer Patterson was obliging and sat down to play whenever she was asked, without nerves or interventions of the ego. St Dunstan's made various demands on her and she rose to the occasion every time, playing by ear, sight-reading, making an attempt on the organ when the organist was away for his summer break. She was a good sort and always wore the right shoes for pedalling. At about four o'clock Paula and Hartley's guests, tired of standing, were becoming soporific with lunchtime drinking. They started to move up to the ground floor and the comforts of sofas and armchairs. Hartley asked Robbie if he would sing. He said he would give it a go. Somebody went to find Jennifer.

Richard remained in the basement, failing to join the guests who were making their way up the stairs, talking and laughing as they went. Because he was feeling lethargic, Richard sat down at the kitchen table. Among the used plates, glasses and platters, two bottles of wine stood, half finished. The catering girls had abandoned the dishes and were occupied with making coffee and tea at the other end of the kitchen. Richard helped himself to the wine, filling up his glass, thinking, cloudily, how pleasant it was to smell coffee and drink alcohol. Better than the opposite, which brought back memories of childhood holidays with his mother and father – car journeys on A roads and the ritual of stopping off for morning coffee in pubs. Morning coffee. The words – the concept – encapsulated those holidays. Always the feeling of prissy isolation, sitting round a small polished table overcrowded with cups and saucers, while the regulars stood at ease by the bar, drinking pints. Afterwards, there was the drama of asking the barman if he would fill up the dog bowl with tap water. *Tap* water, in case the barman decided on another kind, maybe from the soda siphon. His mother would produce the brown earthenware bowl from her bag and hand it over. Once they had been given the water, out they'd all troop, two grown-ups, one boy and a slopping dog bowl. No question of slipping out unobtrusively. The dogs would start to bark as they approached the car, then fall out of the hatchback, wagging their tails, as soon as Father raised the door.

Richard cradled the glass in his hands. The sound of the piano vibrated through the floorboards – the scrape of chairs and thumps made by people shifting about. Robbie's voice was less ample from a distance, but still reverberant. The medley began with 'Sweet By and By', and moved on through 'Amazing Grace' and 'My Shepherd Will Supply My Need'. Richard enjoyed listening from below, happy to suffer the imbalance of instrument and voice for the benefit of not being part of the crowd and, if he were honest, not having to look at the Pattersons. He reached across the table and, although he didn't particularly like hard-boiled quails' eggs, picked up a couple that had been left on a plate and munched them. After a moment's break, Jennifer began playing again. Her hands came down on the keys and – unexpectedly, but as if in response – Richard's head sank down on to the table. Richard, tasting egg in his mouth, heard Robbie's voice through the inebriated roar in his ears.

The catering girls, on the far side of the kitchen, started humming along. They stopped when they noticed Richard, resting on the table, and looked at each other with concern. Then the coffee machine reached its climax and they shrugged their shoulders and got on with counting cups.

3

The phase that Richard hadn't got stuck in was his youthful affair with Jamie Nevis. It had only lasted a few months. Jamie had been different from Richard, less self-conscious, less cautious. Jamie wore sleeveless T-shirts, army trousers and charity shop jackets. He tied a narrow strip of velvet round his right wrist. Richard wore what he considered to be normal clothes – cords and neutral shirts bought from department stores – not actually chosen by his mother, but with her in mind. Richard never told Jamie that he loved him. He believed that he needed to keep checks in place for the sake of his long-term happiness. Richard's parents didn't talk of sexuality, or – much – of love. 'So and so's an attractive woman' was the nearest his father came to it, accompanied by a mild clearing of the throat and a quick glance at his wife, as if the adjective had been an unwise choice. Not everyone was in step, every step of the way, with the prevailing sexual freedoms. There was slippage between social history and personal history, especially in the Epworth family.

Richard was twenty-one and Jamie nineteen when they met. Boys, both of them. Jamie the more clued-up of the two. The meeting took place on the Oxford-to-London bus. Richard had gone home to Abingdon for his mother's birthday – an unavoidable engagement that required him, by custom and practice, to give presents to the two dogs as well as to Mother. He was on his way back to London. He boarded the bus from Oxford bus station at six o'clock on the Sunday evening. The aisle of the bus was crammed with people. Richard waited while individuals in front of him in the queue inserted themselves into the high-backed seats. He found a single space towards the back next to someone with a book open on his knee. Books were generally a good protection against conversation but a short way along the M40 the person – Jamie Nevis – spoke to him. He asked Richard if he knew that Wilde's half-sisters had caught fire. Richard had no idea what he was talking about. He had met people before who suddenly passed on random information. They were usually hoping to make a short art film or had recently started writing a novel. Richard was doped by Sunday lunch, his brain befuddled. Twenty-four hours was the usual recovery period after a home visit. 'I can't believe it,' Jamie said. 'Everyone knows about Reading gaol but no one knows about the sisters. They're getting ready to go to a party, twirling round in front of the fireplace; first one's set alight, then the next.'

'I don't suppose they had a fire extinguisher handy,' Richard said.

Jamie laughed. 'No. They died. I've got half-sisters – in Essex.'

Richard was confused. He looked out of the window across the aisle and beyond the next set of seats. In the dim light he could make out the chalk sides of the hill that the motorway sliced through. No sign of girls carelessly dancing by a log fire. No sign of Reading. He realised who Wilde was, Wilde with an 'e', but it was too late. When he turned back, Jamie's eyes were closed and he had fallen asleep. Richard must have slept too because, apart from odd moments of consciousness when his chin jerked down on to his chest, he didn't wake up until they reached Grosvenor Gardens in Victoria. The bus staggered to a stop. People began to stand up and move forward down the aisle. Richard looked out on to the dark drizzly evening. By nine o'clock on Monday morning he had to have answered a revision question on bounded rationality. 'Short answers will suffice for the micro-economics paper,' his tutor had said. 'But make sure they're spot on.' Richard thought of his room in the student house near the Oval, the dismal programming of Sunday evening television, the lack of beer and clean shirts. He patted the backpack that rested in his lap and, through the canvas, felt the brick-shaped package of foil-wrapped leftovers that had been pressed on him by his mother. Eventually he and Jamie Nevis were the only two left on the bus. The driver began locking up the cash box and operating the winder that changed the bus destination back to Oxford. 'Shall we go somewhere for a drink?' Jamie said.

The glass doors to the Federation, across the river in Vauxhall, were automatic, gliding apart, so there was no hanging around, half in, half out.

'Funny smell,' Jamie said. 'But you get used to it.' The bar had been his choice.

'What is it? Petroleum-based materials? Recently set cement?' Richard asked.

'I don't know,' Jamie said.

'It's supposed to be bad for you, isn't it? New building sickness.'

Jamie inhaled slowly. 'Is it? What's supposed to happen to you?'

'I don't know. Headaches. Asthma. That sort of thing probably.'

'I never get headaches,' Jamie said. 'I never get ill.'

They were walking across the empty floor. The walls to either side rose upwards into blackness. The lighted bar, with a handful of people gathered round it and unoccupied low-level seating to each side, formed a tableau in the distance. Change of use became commonplace later – banks converted to bars and schools to residential blocks – but such transformation seemed sophisticated then. The Federation had only been open a month.

'Extraordinary place,' Richard said. 'Like a cathedral. Everything happening at the far end.'

'A working men's club, not a cathedral. They stripped the inside out and made it over. I like it,' Jamie said. 'Weird music, though. Haven't you been here?' He moved away from Richard, stretched out his arms horizontally and turned round slowly, completing a circle. That was the first time Richard really noticed Jamie's clothes, the narrow strip of velvet round his right wrist.

They were three-quarters of the way through their second pint of beer when Jamie glanced at his watch. It was a nice old sixties Ingersoll that had to be wound. Jamie had already shown it to Richard. He had found it at a boot fair in Essex, near where his family lived. It turned out that he and Richard were both at London University, though at different colleges, reading different subjects. They had swapped information about student life and cheap eating places. Richard had been describing the birthday weekend, meaning to make it sound funny. Jamie had laughed, out of sympathy, not because he found the story amusing. Then the talk petered out. The corner seat where they were sitting was in shadow, dark enough for the luminous paint on the watch numbers to glow. The watch showed half past ten.

'Say something,' Richard said, staring into the glass.

'How do you usually meet people?' Jamie said rather loudly.

Richard downed his beer. He knew Jamie didn't mean people. 'I don't.'

'There are no hidden microphones.'

'I'm not gay,' Richard said.

'Don't worry about it.'

'Do you want something else to drink?' Richard asked, after a few moments of silence.

'No, thank you.' Jamie got to his feet.

'It hasn't been a great conversation on my part. I'm sorry,' Richard said.

Jamie smiled and shrugged his shoulders. 'It was all right.'

Richard stood up too. He put on his coat and buttoned it. Doing up buttons makes some people look like children. Perhaps it's the way they do it. They show a sort of concentration that makes them look vulnerable. For some reason Richard saw that in himself and fixed the particular image in his mind. He still remembered it, nearly twenty years later, though other pictures that he would have preferred to retain had gone for ever. He picked up his backpack containing the bag of leftovers. But then he was reluctant to move.

'Shall we go?' Jamie said.

'Where?' The question seemed to come from nowhere.

'Mine?' Jamie said.

When Jamie was dying, Richard promised God he'd give him up. It wasn't a wager – not an either/or promise. He made it when the message got through to him that Jamie was in University College Hospital with acute viral meningitis. If Jamie had survived the terrible fever it would have held, and if he had died, inescapably, the same. The promise needed to be unconditional. It was as if he had been trying to impose a counterweight to Jamie's soaring temperature; a strike for equilibrium. Richard hadn't, at that time, been conspicuously Christian – just timidly and conventionally brought up. He hadn't 'closed the deal' as Paula and Hartley would have said – or prayed the prayer asking Jesus to come into his life. That had come later after he had started going out with Vivienne. The emergency appeal to God, at the time of Jamie's illness, had somehow been primitive, straight from the gut. He had wanted to give something – out of love – and that was all he had to give. The willed attempt at forgetting had begun then. It was the only way he could cope. After returning from the funeral – a dreamlike assembling of strangers and friends at a crematorium in Essex – Richard looked one last time at the photographs. There were twelve of them, in a yellow Kodak packet, all taken on a day trip to Brighton. He walked to Vauxhall Bridge and threw them into the Thames. Richard had never visited Jamie's family – they were among the strangers – and as far as he knew, no one had ever guessed that he and Jamie were lovers.

Richard survived the turbulent period after Jamie's death, though at the time he didn't care about survival. All his everyday actions slowed down, and split into moments of time so tenuous that the days and nights were endless and their shape unrecognisable. He took to his bed at unsuitable times. He moved slowly and aimlessly. He nearly said inappropriate things. He felt on the point of tears. It was as if he were trapped in a lift, with his own thoughts blaring out from an intercom. He let it be known that a friend had died suddenly. He implied an *old* friend, though he and Jamie had only known each other for a short time. Nothing less than an *old* friend would have explained his sadness. Of all his circle, Paula and Hartley showed the least alarm. They made their way to the Oval at regular and dependable intervals; brought food, tidied his room, opened windows. They talked to his parents and tutors on his behalf, and tuned out the worried sounds from their messages before they relayed them back to Richard. When Richard revived enough to listen, and even when he barely listened, Paula and Hartley told him who had sent their love and who had been praying for him – all in the same reassuring tone of voice. He came to appreciate these benign communiqués that involved no evident obligation. It was like a return to childhood: receiving Christmas and birthday presents from people he didn't know.

He couldn't put a date to a week, or even a month, when he knew he was better. Over time, tiredness became bearable tiredness and anxiety merged with boredom. The waves of grief grew further apart. He managed to sit his final exams. He went on a walking holiday in the Pyrenees. He became articled to a firm of accountants. Paula introduced him to Vivienne and when they became engaged he joined St

Dunstan's. He came to believe in the power of prayer which, combined with some dependable resilience of his own, saw him through.

4

Richard had shut up the Abe episode in a box that he was determined never to open. As a husband and a Christian, he was appalled at what had happened, but the part of him that was pure Epworth pragmatist considered that the best way to deal with the encounter was to vow that it would never happen again and forget about it. This worked for a week or so, but through February and March, different breaches occurred in Richard's defences, old memories and new fantasies. Richard could hardly distinguish them. Their comfort as mental relief was compromised by his inability to control them. Abe, or men resembling Abe, walked into his thoughts: young men with springy hair and an easy way of talking. Then there was more to control, because the spectres also had to be extinguished. After the family returned home from skiing, Richard avoided the guest bedroom where he and Abe had slept – though sometimes all he wanted to do was to go in and lie quietly on the bed.

There were layers of permission in his fantasies that were like interleaves. Richard came across them: thin, almost opaque, sheets between one page of his thoughts and the next. To steady himself, he kept returning to the weather on that January evening. Epworths could cope with weather. But the topic blew itself out and he moved on to the chance encounter, the way Abe had arrived at his house. It had been simple but also complicated – like a dream mixed up with a weird mathematical probability problem. What was the likelihood of something like that happening? The timing soothed him – the way the flow had created itself. He remembered Abe's careless questions about the girls, and his own anxious queasiness as he heard them spoken of. He had replied to the questions. The queasiness passed. His best memory was of Abe, in the darkness of the taxi, with his hands clasped behind the back of his head, his legs stretching across the taxi floor – the posture of businessmen when feigning contemplation.

Richard had taken the sheets to the express laundry. He had checked and rechecked the guest bedroom and bathroom – believing that he was bound either to have missed or created some domestic discrepancy that Vivienne would home in on. On the correct day he turned up at Heathrow Airport, joining the po-faced men behind the rope at Arrivals who were carrying boards or makeshift notices bearing wonkily inscribed names. He scanned the incoming passengers emerging from the Customs Hall and saw his wife and daughters before they saw him. In that split second he panicked at not being recognised – afraid that he had turned into a stranger. Then the girls started grinning and waving. They came running towards him. Vivienne, tussling with the luggage on wheels, finally noticed him. By the time she reached him and he was hugging her, he had forgotten the blank look on her face that suggested he might not have been her husband.

His blunder, it turned out, had been failing to take down the Christmas decorations. He had got into trouble for that – past Twelfth Night, past Epiphany. Vivienne had said that they had never left Christmas decorations up beyond the due date. Richard claimed that he had lived entirely in the kitchen and the bedroom while she and the girls were away. He said he had forgotten to go into the other rooms. Vivienne had nodded, as if she believed him, but it was clear that she felt exposed. To what, Richard wasn't quite sure. Bad luck didn't come into it. Or good luck. In the circumstances he felt unable to press the point. He looked on while Vivienne stripped the dried-up tree. First the decorations, then the lights, which she unwound, beginning at the top, until she had a tangle of green wire and tiny bulbs festooned round one arm. A pile of crisp pine needles collected on the floor and yet more fell into the decorations box, which had once contained the computer printer and still bore its name and outline on the side. Having pulled the plug from the socket, Vivienne placed the tangle in the top of the box and pushed down the flaps. Richard had closed his ears to the possible scrunch. Vivienne had looked up at him rather defiantly and said that if it turned out that the lights had shattered, they would simply have to go to John Lewis next December and buy new.

Several times Richard came close to dialling the mobile number Abe had given him and which he had committed to memory. He had looked at it often enough to have it by heart. He wanted to hear Abe's voice – the deadpan delivery that suddenly activated. The thought of Abe answering the phone in person stopped him. Since he hadn't made the call, what did 'coming close to' mean? He could make no sense of the words that he used to describe his unguarded intentions; it pained him to use them.

So far, his work hadn't been affected but weariness, free time, ordinary days at home laid him open. Richard valued his family. For him it came first. Fractures to his contentment, during the twelve years of his marriage, had been infrequent; caused by a look, a touch that changed the rhythm of his thoughts. He had never acted on the strange uneasiness that came over him, so there was nothing to remind him once the moment had passed. The notion of Men Seeking Men in the personal columns, or by any other means, was as alien to him as the equivalent Men Seeking Women. He disapproved of affairs between married men and their secretaries, or female colleagues, and he would have disapproved of an affair between a married man and another man even more, if he had heard of such a thing in the office. He wasn't, and never had been, on the lookout. It was as if he were on a bridge which he knew to be safe, well above the waterline, when, for no reason that he could understand or predict, he felt the bridge breaking. Until meeting Abe he had held steady.

On the afternoon of Easter Monday Richard drove up to Harrow-on-the-Hill to drop off Bethany and Martha at a birthday party. The village, as people called it, was only a mile or so away from where the Epworths lived but, apart from delivering the girls to social events, Richard had little reason to go there. He hadn't been for over a year; certainly not since January.

Richard knew that he had reached the right house when he saw the red and orange balloons attached to the gatepost, the 4x4s, pavement-parked, and children clambering down from them. He let the girls out of the car and they ran across the gravelled drive and in through a door with a fanlight above it. Decent-sized family houses 'on-the-Hill' were out of his price bracket, which was why he and Vivienne had ended up with a less desirable postcode, off Sudbury Hill, in one of the new executive homes that backed on to the grounds of a private hospital. Compared with some of his colleagues in the City, his income was modest. He never got the huge bonuses. No one did in his department. It was a backwater that had, so far, escaped being the focus of an initiative.

As he had taken no exercise at all on Easter Day and was still feeling thick-headed from Paula's lunch, Richard decided that rather than drive home and set out again later he would go for a walk. Having manoeuvred the car into a proper parking space, he left a message for Vivienne, explaining what he was doing, then switched off his phone. He got out and locked the car door. He looked up and down the street as he inserted coins in the meter. There was a woman on a bicycle and a man with a dog; no one he recognised.

Meeting anyone by chance always gave Richard a jolt – like the time he had met a colleague's secretary, Tricia, at the customer services desk at the Marks and Spencer at Finsbury Pavement and had suddenly found himself explaining why he was returning the pack of socks in his hand. Turning a corner and coming across Abe would have immobilised him. He would have felt an agonising level of embarrassment and come out with some idiotic remark. No, he wasn't expecting to meet Abe.

Richard walked down the high street, pausing to look at the headless models in the window of the school outfitter's. They posed against wood panels, in their blazers and trousers, rugby shirts and shorts – personifications of right conduct that wouldn't last once they got a boy inside them. The atmosphere of Harrow had always seemed to him stifling, in spite of its airy position. The inescapable school buildings – the aesthetic mix of guest house and nineteenth-century town prison – made the village feel enclosed.

Abe and Kirsty's living arrangements had charmed him – the anachronism. The old-fashioned house share with a sibling and the unapologetic way Abe had announced it meant a lot to him. People sometimes go back to live with their parents but not many join up with a brother or sister for a second bout. It had been good to discover that not everyone in their twenties conformed to the same pattern – Richard had lagged behind himself, in various departments, at that age. His choice of music, films and clothes had been dull. Sub-optimal. Only his willingness to learn – and please – had saved him. And then, once he was married, Vivienne's good taste and influence.

Richard guessed that Kirsty must be a good earner, probably older than Abe and generous enough to give her brother a helping hand financially. Even so, their house must be small – two and a half beds at the most – because property prices in the village were high. He wondered what Kirsty looked like and if he would see enough family resemblance to know her if he passed her in the street. Remembering the mother's peculiar Egyptian hobby, he somehow imagined the daughter as black-haired and carefully made up around the eyes. Richard allowed himself a few uncomplicated pictures of Abe: happy ones, different from the troubling images that plagued him at home. They were like old-style holiday snaps. Abe in a thick jersey wearing his beanie hat and balancing an upturned broom on the flat of his hand. Abe shaking the snow from the silver fir tree under a bright blue sky – cheery snow scenes pictures. They were set in his garden and had never happened. These thoughts went round his head, about Abe and the sister, but somehow missing the point – skirting round his awkward feelings of longing and guilt. He caught sight of himself in the glass of another shop, a middle-aged man wearing pale jeans and a dark shirt; dressed down for bank holiday, lacking the usual weekday suit.

Richard climbed up to the churchyard and self-consciously admired the view, then, taking a steep footpath down again, he headed for the quiet residential roads on the western slope of the hill where the houses were more modest. He was enjoying his walk. He told himself that the advantages of building on a hill are the changes of level: unexpected juxtapositions, roofs and chimneys below, front gardens looking up. This was as true in Harrow as in Tuscany. He concentrated on outward things. Richard made no claims to possessing an artist's eye, but today he appreciated the way buildings fitted together. His instinct, when going along a street, was to estimate property prices to the nearest five thousand pounds. He made the usual appraisal now but, with time on his hands, he went on to look in a less mercantile way – at houses through windows. He imagined the inhabitants and paid attention to the faces he passed. He realised what little notice he took of his own neighbourhood – getting into the car, pulling out of the drive – and why Vivienne was sometimes incredulous at his inadequate observation.

As Richard walked along, the motion of his steps and the shafts of weak sunshine that appeared between the roofs put him in good spirits. He felt less rushed than for weeks and seemed to be acquiring another, calmer identity. He imagined returning to the Hill on future occasions. He decided that whenever the girls needed to be ferried to parties or French club he would drop them off, drive over to Harrow, park the car on the lower slopes, where he wouldn't be clamped, and have a wander around until it was time to collect them. He might try one of the pubs for a pint of beer, or even have a haircut.

He was passing a row of flat-fronted Victorian cottages when an old fellow with a walking stick addressed him. 'Rain's holding off for you,' he said. Richard agreed. He was pleased to be greeted. A few minutes later he heard a woman singing. It was an unselfconscious, private sound and came from inside one of the cottages. The song was unaccompanied – perfect to his ears. Richard didn't slow down. He went on to the end of the road, then retraced his steps. The singing had stopped by the time he returned. Richard scanned the front of the cottage – only two storeys high, he could take it in at a glance. Number twelve was similar to the others in the street; built of yellow London stock bricks with three windows – all open, two up, one down – and a solid-looking front door. There was a bicycle and a wheelie bin in the narrow front yard. A solitary pot containing a small shrub, tipped with brown leaves, stood by the path. The gate was broken, tied to its hinges by a piece of wire. In the window of the front room was a stone cat, tall and regal, Egyptian-looking, even with its back turned. Its ears strained upwards, as if tracking a flock of birds flying overhead. Seeing the cat, Richard flinched, as if he'd been slapped round the head. His shirt went damp under his arms and across his back.

He walked down the hill and made his way to the car. He unlocked the door and almost crawled into the driver's seat. He felt contained sitting there, soothed by the familiar smell of the leather seats, the arrangement of the dashboard, the leftover twirl of paper from a roll of Extra Strong Mints in the dip between the two front seats. He was aware that the association of singing and a stone cat was random, and that there was nothing logical or causal linking them. The overwhelming feeling that he was standing in front of Abe's house had come more from his pulse – which was only now slowing down – and a buzzing in his brain, than from any rational explanation. He didn't move until a traffic warden tapped on the window and pointed at the meter. Then he nodded, put on his seat belt, turned the key in the ignition and drove away.

Julian's mother was very understanding when Richard turned up nearly half an hour after the party had ended. All the other children had already been collected. Richard apologised and Julian's mother went to call the girls. The hall he waited in was splendid, like the entrance to a house people pay to look around. The paintings were lit with individual lights in the form of brass shells, and the walls were covered in some silky cloth. He stood and gaped, at a loss without a ticket. At a loss altogether. Bethany and Martha were watching a DVD, finishing the birthday cake. Julian's mother hurried them out, ignoring the crumbs that they shed as they ran across the huge Chinese rug. No one made Julian come and say goodbye. He was said to be upstairs getting into his combats, preparing to go to the RAF museum at Hendon for the birthday treat.

5

Someone told Abe that Declan Driscol was on a concert tour of Germany, but he couldn't have been because Abe saw him one evening on the Festival Terrace at the South Bank. A crowd of mesmerised passers-by had gathered in a semicircle round him and another group were sitting on the steps of Hungerford footbridge. Abe joined the outer part of the circle and looked on. Declan's long fingers were buckled over his recorder. He sucked in his cheeks until they nearly touched. Abe liked Pachelbel's Canon – the eight notes that repeated for ever – but he felt apart from whatever was drawing the crowd. He kept his mouth closed and hummed along, 'Declan Driscol still owes me a fiver; Declan Driscol still owes ... ' He hadn't seen Declan for months. He had left Iverdale Road one day and never come back. Declan had once spoken of 'the path to improvisation'. Abe supposed he was now on it – whatever it was.

Abe was in a strange mood. The house-warming period had come to an end. He couldn't afford to give any more parties. He couldn't afford to go out. He had overspent. For the first time since he was about eight years old he stopped thinking about sex in a spirit of curiosity – when and how it would happen. At home, he set fire to small bits of paper in ashtrays – pieces of till roll that had ended up in his pocket, receipts and tube tickets. Declan's dusty Irish drifter looks, as he played his recorder by the Thames, had no effect on him. Abe felt as unresponsive as a piece of old toast.

*

Needing to do something real, Abe gave in his notice to the health insurance company. His meeting with the boss was a waste of time – not worth psyching himself up for. Liam was genial and nodded to show he was listening. He didn't try to persuade Abe to stay or insist he take gardening leave. He smiled when he opened the door to show Abe out and gave him a comradely cuff on the back. Abe wandered across to the lift, got out at the third floor and walked back to his office. That was it: over like a jab at the doctor's. Four years ended in five minutes. Holly came across and hugged him and said that if he was going she would quit too. Then she went off to a meeting. Ben had already left for a presentation in the Midlands.

Abe expected to feel elated at the prospect of freedom but instead he found himself living in a kind of border zone, which he wasn't allowed to leave and where very little went on. He commuted to Reading from Monday to Friday as usual, but every day he felt as if he had made a bad choice of holiday – arriving in a grey place in dull weather. In less than a month he would be gone. Away from the pictures of tanned young men lying on daybeds in their boxer shorts and Grandma doing a more than competent star jump in a pair of bright pyjamas – those fit types who sexed up not only the client brochures but also the company documents, the interior walls of the building, the inside of the lift. He wanted to scrawl BOLLOCKS across them with an indelible pen. He wondered whether car insurance might not, in fact, be a cleaner sort of business. At least no one ever suggested that cars enjoyed going in for repair.

The Saturday after Abe had resigned, Gloria asked herself over to Iverdale Road. She turned up in the afternoon. Abe went into the kitchen to make some tea and when he came back, holding two mugs, Gloria was sitting very upright, perched on the edge of his sumptuous vintage swivel chair. Abe had bought the chair in Hoxton. It was velvety, the colour of blackberries and covered in silvery diamond-shaped stitching. Gloria wasn't taking advantage of the chair's swivelling properties. 'You're in debt, aren't you?' she said. 'Anyway.'

Abe knew Gloria's habit of asking a question as if she were a telephone waking him in the night, but he was still caught off guard. 'I've got a loan from the bank. Don't worry about it. I spoke to a woman and it's cool.' He handed her one of the mugs.

'Thank you. What was her name?'

'Whose name?'

'The woman at the bank.'

Abe walked across the room and sat down heavily on the sofa. 'I don't know. Gemma or something. Yes, I think it was Gemma,' he said.

Gloria always wanted to know everyone's name. It came from teaching and dealing with the public. Without names you were shouting into the wind. Gloria worked at a beauty treatment centre and had certificates to prove her competence in laser hair removal, non-surgical face lifts, waxing, piercing. She also taught in local authority adult education classes. 'Singing for Everyone' it was called in the brochure. She had been a singer once – folk and jazz – and had done a few festivals. 'Everyone' was the category Abe fell into. He could sing *along* but not sing. If his mum and sister were in any sense artists, he was stuck with the colouring in.

'She was nice to you, was she? Helpful?' Gloria asked, with an edge to her voice.

'Yes, really nice,' he said.

'Do you have credit cards, Abe?'

'Only a couple. They're not a problem.'

Gloria suited the chair: tiny and symmetrical in the centre of it, her feet, in a pair of red leather boots, neatly lined up and barely touching the floor. Though slight, with a skin like thin ice, she had always been as strong as two parents combined. When he was a little boy Abe had focused on her blemishes. The freckle on her left cheekbone that was larger than the general peppering on her translucent skin, the bottom front teeth that slightly overlapped, the scar on the back of her head that she had acquired from falling backwards off a wall and which Abe had only been able to find by pulling different sections of her hair apart at the roots. But since he had stopped examining her so closely he had seen that she was, for a human being, remarkably harmonious. Only cats stared at you with such levelness.

'You look sweet sitting there, Mum,' he said. 'I might give you that chair.'

'Have you even *looked* for another job?' she asked.

''Course I have. I've got all sorts of ideas.'

'Anything real?'

'Well, obviously nothing definite, because travelling up and down to Reading and working all day long I can't go looking in a *real* way.' He paused. 'This is really tedious. Can we stop talking about it?'

Gloria's only mushiness had started in New Age bookshops. She browsed in several sections, including channelling, crystals and subtle energy. She collected magical and spiritual texts. They originated from various sources, Egyptian, Celtic, Native American. On balance, Gloria favoured the Egyptian. She set the words to chants and practised her singing on them – musical sun salutations – up and down the keys. She answered ads in esoteric magazines to gather more material: *Harness the Power of Ba*, *Heart-weighing: are you ready for it?*, *Hen kai pan: beginners welcome (we're all beginners!)*. The leaflets turned up in her house, slipped behind radiators or wedged in the windows as draught preventers. Abe thought the hobby was barmy but he understood that a person can't be strong in every area of life. Something has to give.

'How's the chanting going?' Abe asked.

Gloria ignored him. 'Why are you stopping work, Abe?'

'No particular reason. I've been there long enough. Four years.'

'You worry me.'

'Don't waste your time, Mum.'

'Don't waste yours.' Gloria got up from the chair and started wandering around the room. Her boots were flat with soft soles and hardly made a sound as she walked across the boards. Abe saw her twice over, once in reality and once reflected in the huge, driftwood-framed mirror that covered one wall. The window frames were rotting; it was depressing to see an extra set of them. Certain aspects of the Iverdale Road house were starting to grate on Abe. His pieces of furniture, from interesting parts of London, deserved better than the tatty shell that contained them. It was like having a mouth full of expensive dentistry in a scarred, sunken face.

Gloria didn't glance at her reflection. For someone who worked part-time in the beauty trade she was surprisingly unconcerned about looks. Nor, at that moment, did she seem interested in Abe's daybed or matt nickel floor lights – his last purchases before the money ran out. Abe had tidied up before she arrived. He had collected up the ashtrays, full of charred pieces of paper. There was nothing out of place.

Gloria picked up one of the lemons that was lying in a black enamelled bowl on the table, rubbed it between her hands and sniffed it. 'Abe, is there a cigarette?' she asked.

'Yes. I'll get you one. Sit down, Mum,' he said. He went out of the room and came back with a single cigarette and a lighter. He threw them over to her one at a time. She caught them and stood contemplating him.

'I go to Reading every single day,' he said. 'Even though I've given in my notice. Sometimes I feel like the office poltergeist, not truly there and banging into things. But I never miss.'

'Congratulations,' she said.

'I agree. I'm fantastic.'

'A fantasist, did you say?' She lit the cigarette and, after a meditative in-breath, turned her head and exhaled away from where Abe was standing. The hand that she waved to one side was decorated with silver rings; the tips of her fingernails painted pearly white.

He remembered how she used to light her cigarettes from the front burner on the gas stove. She saw herself as an occasional smoker and never had matches or lighters. These were for addicts, not singers. When he was very young, she used to dance him round the living room on her shoulders, arms outstretched – flying, she called it. She sang as she danced and he heard the vibrations of sound coming out from the top of her head. On one occasion she was singing Joni Mitchell's song 'Carey' and stopped in midline when Abe screamed. He had grabbed her hands and one of them was holding a cigarette. No one reached the Mermaid Café that day. A blister as big as a soap bubble came up in the middle of his palm.

'But afterwards, Abe. When you *have* left. Don't waste your time,' Gloria said.

''Course not. 'Course not, Mum. That's why I'm giving up work.'

She didn't reply but her pencil-thin eyebrows moved, as if her brain were still having its say, although she, for reasons of her own, had decided to keep quiet. That was probably it, Abe thought, for the ticking off. He hoped she wouldn't leave. She had only been there half an hour.

'Shall I get my head shaved? What do you think?' Abe smoothed his hands back from his forehead in an attempt to show how he would look with no hair.

'If you like,' Gloria said without even studying him. He never could engage her, only if he transgressed and then she was as alert as if she had spotted a hornet in the room. Once or twice a year he went back to Crystal Palace. He liked dipping into the old atmosphere – as if he were climbing into a familiar bath, then realising how cool the water had become. The decreasing temperature was part of the pleasure. His old bedroom had become storage, like one of those industrial cubes people rented. Gloria's winter coat with its fake-fur collar and cuffs hung in his cupboard in summer and her floaty summer clothes, in burnished seventies colours, hung there in winter, together with the portable massage table, from the days when she had treated clients at home. But then he looked up and saw the lampshade. Same old red lampshade from Habitat, circa 1980, that had dangled there from the beginning – familiar as the moon but without waxing or waning. He felt nostalgic thinking about it. 'Are you going to see Kirsty?' he asked.

'Is she in? She sometimes works on Saturday at that privatised post office.'

'I don't know. We could call her, ask her up.' Abe picked up his phone and went over to the window. 'She's not answering.'

'One of you on the dole and the other selling stamps,' Gloria said.

When Abe turned round he saw that she had sat down on the swivel chair again. She had stubbed out the cigarette and retrieved the lemon. She was passing it from hand to hand.

'Would you like some more tea, Mum?' he asked.

'Abe,' she said.

'Yes?'

'Gemma.'

For a moment, Abe didn't know who she was talking about. 'Oh, you're not on about the bank again, are you?'

'She isn't being nice or helpful. She is digging a pit and her sole aim and purpose is that you fall in it.'

'That's a bit of an exaggeration, isn't it? Stop worrying, Mum.'

Gloria said no to the tea – she was never big on tea – but she stayed ten minutes longer. After she had gone, Abe decided to meet Kirsty from work. He hadn't seen her for a while. He missed her.

Abe caught a bus to the West End and walked along the backstreets away from the crowds. He hadn't lost the habit of noticing men but it was an empty sport; more like watching nature programmes on TV than getting to know the tigers. He thought, with a touch of nostalgia, of his trip to Sudbury Hill. He remembered the snow. He wished another random journey might present itself. Richard had mentioned 'meeting up again', but that wasn't what Abe had in mind. He didn't plan to see Richard again.

Abe resolved to respond to the next man who showed a flicker of interest but in the ten minutes that followed he met no one, not even a traffic warden. He found the mail box premises and opened the door. Abe shared the view that his sister lacked ambition but he hadn't reckoned with the effect of seeing Kirsty standing behind a counter under an international clock that gave the time in distant cities. She looked even slighter than usual in an oversized grey jumper which she wore with a string of iridescent beads. Her motive for suddenly dressing up as an aggregated gran and grandad, when she had the body of an elf, was a mystery to Abe. For a second he felt moved. He went to the far end of the shop and examined the stock on the shelves. The packing materials gave off a dead brown smell. He suspected that Kirsty enjoyed arranging the stationery in harmonious groups – comforted by the orderliness of ascending sizes of padded envelopes and the geometry of the flat-pack boxes. Some of the customers would have the same fetish. They would finger the goods but leave them tidy.

Several fat rolls of bubble wrap were propped up against the shelves. Abe peeled off a corner of the protecting wrapping and, pressing his thumb between the layers, popped a bubble. The noise it made was like the click of a door. Abe looked towards the counter to see if he had attracted Kirsty's attention. Kirsty remained oblivious but the customer she was serving glanced over his shoulder. The man smiled at Abe. He was of what the police call 'Mediterranean' appearance, black-haired with neatly shaped fuzz in front of his ears. Abe smiled too. The man raised a finger discreetly, in mock admonition. Abe walked back to the counter. 'She doesn't mind. She's my sister,' he said.

'Your sister?' The man's eyes moved from Abe to Kirsty and back.

'Yes. She's beautiful, isn't she?'

'Very beautiful. Maybe she will give me free photocopying.'

'She's my sister, not yours.'

The man laughed. Kirsty set her face into a cross mask. 'It is good that you have such a brother,' the man said, peeling a fifty-pound note from a wad in his wallet. 'He looks after you good.' He leant across the counter and proffered his hand. After the scant shake that Kirsty allowed him, the man turned to Abe. He gathered up Abe's hands in both of his. Abe smelled peppery hair oil as the man leant towards him. 'Thank you. Thank you. Very pleased to meet you. I will see you again. I am often here with the photocopying.'

'Nice to meet you, too.' Abe released his hands from the small butter-smooth ones. He walked over to the door of the shop and held it open. The man touched Abe's arm and went out into the street. Abe returned to the counter.

Kirsty's arms were folded inside the overlarge jumper. Her hands had disappeared. 'Thanks, Abe. You've just made my life a whole lot easier.'

'That's all right.'

'What are you doing here, anyway?'

'I wanted to see you.'

They locked eyes, as if playing a game of who blinks first. Abe was the one to give in.

'Why do you come on to pathetic random people, Abe? What's the point of it?'

'I never came on to him,' Abe protested. 'I never did a thing.' He held up his hands.

Kirsty took a breath. 'I do my best here, Abe. I try out my school French. I've bought an Arabic phrase book to help work out what people want. I'm polite and they're polite and, from time to time, when they invite me to go out with them in their cars they are extra polite and make it easy for me to refuse them.'

'All right,' Abe said. 'Why are you telling me this?'

'I'm just trying to explain that it's better if no one gets excited.'

Abe shrugged his shoulders. 'Fair enough. But that's their problem, isn't it? If they get excited?'

Kirsty turned away from him. She looked genuinely fed up, which wasn't what he had intended.

'Cheer up, Kirstabel. Let's go and have a drink.' He didn't want her to cry.

'I can't, Abe. I can't leave before six.' A tear was halfway down her cheek.

'Tomorrow, then. Let's go and have a Sunday roast. We haven't been out for ages.'

'Sorry,' Kirsty said. She paused. 'I've asked Luka round.'

'Are you two back together?' Abe said.

'No,' she said, wiping her hand across her face.

Abe let out a long breath. 'And you accuse me of making trouble?'

6

In their more companionable daytime moments Abe and Kirsty talked of getting a cat. They talked of different types and colours of cat, and chose a short list of names. Those were good conversations. Then Abe was given two fish in a tank as a late house-warming present and they postponed the cat plan. The fish started off in Abe's bedroom – swimming there – but it was stuffy under the roof and the water evaporated too fast. The plants went brown and slimy. Abe either overfed the fish or forgot to feed them at all. He breathed dope over them. Kirsty felt sorry for them and brought them downstairs. They lived happily in her cool kitchen from then on and made beautiful moving shadows on the blue walls.

Nothing much happened with the fish, apart from the ritual of catching them in the net and flipping them into the glass salad bowl, in order to clean the tank. On these occasions Kirsty filled up the bowl with tepid tap water so as not to give them a shock. They swam round and round, bored and shitting, unaware of the lettuce and vinaigrette they were replacing. It wasn't much of a holiday, more of an endurance test – for her, as well as for them. Once they came downstairs, they were her responsibility, though Abe still referred to them as his. Remembering the goldfish in her primary school, Kirsty fed them every morning before she put the kettle on for a cup of tea. She made a few smacking kissing noises and said good morning. Sometimes she sang to them in her clear voice. They could listen if they wanted to. She topped up their water, pouring it from a jug into a saucer held under the surface, so that the gravel at the bottom wouldn't be disturbed. And she cleaned the tank. She had enough to do without the fish, but they were alive and she didn't want them to die. She was rather resentful of the time they took up – though it wasn't a lot – and, in the way of things, this meant they took up more time, both the time itself and the time spent feeling resentful, which didn't necessarily, or usually, coincide.

Since splitting up with Luka, Kirsty had become more solitary. She no longer met up with her friends several times a week. 'I love you, Kirst. You don't piss around, like the rest of us,' Marlene said. 'I really admire that. Let me be the first to hear your new songs when you're ready.' Kirsty wasn't. She wished Marlene wouldn't mention new songs. There was only one and it didn't exist. In her free time Kirsty walked around the side streets or to one of the nearby parks, Roundwood, Brondesbury, Gladstone. She liked their sturdy names. She went, not to orientate herself, but to see her surroundings while they were still strange, because that moment never comes again. The early spring weather was gloomy but she enjoyed those walks. The leaves that had fallen in the autumn were still piled up on the pathways. They looked crisp and old. Kirsty couldn't match any of these parks to the one that Neil had taken them to when they were little. It was always 'the park' and they went in Neil's car. He drove fast through streets lined with small houses, as if he knew for certain that there would be no children or cats playing there. She must have been nervous, because once they had run over an old grey raincoat and she had screamed and screamed. Neil had pulled in to the kerb and turned the engine off – had just sat there. Abe, in the back of the car, hadn't said a word. When she was quiet, Neil had said calmly, looking straight ahead, 'Don't ever make that noise in my car again. Do you want to cause a fucking accident?'

She remembered that the park toilets were embedded in a tall dark hedge and that the floor of the Ladies, where she had to go without Abe, was always flooded with oily-looking water. The toilet paper was reduced to a cardboard roll and the basin was untouchable. There was a playground slide with a glass-smooth finish and sides that were sharp enough to cut your hands on, if you held on to them on the descent. The see-saw was broken. Permanently up – or down – depending how you looked at it. Kirsty was disappointed with herself for not remembering more and wondered what else she had forgotten.

As she often had to work on Saturdays, Kirsty rarely had two free days in a row. Single days off were precious so she guarded them. Sometimes she guarded them so closely that nothing happened. Sometimes she felt lonely. She had received four or five text messages from Luka since they had split up and, as none of them sounded desperate, she had decided to ask him over. Sunday lunch would be best, she thought. Kirsty offered Luka a few dates and he accepted the first available.

He turned up on the doorstep with a bottle of wine. There were three buses backing up from the traffic lights, juddering and burning up diesel oil outside the house, so Kirsty didn't quite catch what he said after he'd said hello. Luka kissed her on the cheek. His face was damp and cold. He felt alien – even exotic – and she wondered how it would feel to have his face next to hers every day, forgetting for an instant that, until recently, she had done. Kirsty closed the door behind him and the buses showed red through the ridged glass.

As soon as they were in the kitchen, Kirsty opened the bottle. She had done some of the preparation in advance – chopping up the peppers and making a salad dressing; there was only the chicken to grill. She turned on the extractor fan over the stove and the noise was a refuge for her because she didn't have to talk or to listen to the silence. She could pretend that she and Luka were friends and the extractor fan was on.

She said the food was ready. They sat at the kitchen table at right angles to each other – a jug full of daffodils between them – the brightest thing in the room – and the talk didn't flow, in spite of the wine, which by then was almost gone. Kirsty had made an orange polenta cake and asked Luka if he'd like a cup of coffee with it but he said no, he'd rather not wake up. He had a cigarette instead. He fiddled around making a roll-up, scattering shreds of tobacco on the floor, then went over to the creaky sash window and forced it wide open because he knew Kirsty didn't like smoking indoors. The room became cold in a few minutes and the warm citrus smell of the cake drifted away. Luka rested his wrists on the frame and blew smoke into the garden. Upstairs, the front door slammed and Kirsty heard the bump bump of bicycle wheels on the steps. She sat at the table, staring at Luka's back, wishing she hadn't turned down Abe's invitation to Sunday lunch in a pub.

'Shall we go for a walk?' she said.

'If you want,' Luka said.

They went to Roundwood Park. Luka walked on the kerb side and kept his hands in his pockets. He was wearing his oldest trainers and a pair of tartan socks that Kirsty hadn't seen before. There had been repairs to the gas pipes the previous week. The pavement had been dug up and put back haphazardly, leaving seams of tarmac in sticky footpaths. About halfway up the street, a pigeon landed a metre or so in front of them and carried on wobbling fast ahead like an automaton, as if it had forgotten it could fly.

'Are the birds round here thick or something?' Luka said. He lunged forward and stamped his foot. Kirsty yelped. The pigeon raised itself off the ground with a few flaps and veered into the road as a car was passing. Kirsty shut her eyes. She felt the squelch but when she dared to look she saw the pigeon alive and pecking in the gutter.

As soon they were inside the park gates, Kirsty wished they had gone somewhere else. Roundwood Park wasn't a place you could get lost in, but she saw at a glance that it had shrunk since she had last been there.

'Do you *like* it here?' Luka said.

'Yes,' she said, rallying. 'I do. It's a perfect curve – like a microcosm of the earth's surface.'

The park was surrounded by low houses and backed on to two cemeteries – the Willesden New Cemetery and the Jewish Reformed Cemetery – but the rounded hill was special. The top of the curve was marked out by a circle of trees and through them, looking westwards, you could see the tilting structure of the new Wembley Stadium arch and the tower blocks of Neasden. Kirsty liked the view, which wasn't of great interest and would never have appeared on a calendar. She liked the bland horizon and all the ordinary houses stretching towards it.

Luka nodded, though not in response to her answer. He nodded as if he were very wise and she had confirmed something detrimental to her that he already knew. His eyes didn't look wise, though. They looked belligerent.

Kirsty and Luka made a single circuit of the park, which took about ten minutes, then Luka said he was going to find the tube station. He headed off in the wrong direction, his collar up, his hands in his pockets, but Kirsty didn't call after him.

I made him like that, she thought, as she walked back to Iverdale Road. There was nothing horrible about him and now there is. He was the type who would have gone on, for years, being all right, neither better nor worse, like a packet of sugar at the back of the cupboard. She had met him at a former cinema in New Cross. She was singing in a charity event, dressed in a low-cut black T-shirt and a bronze-coloured tiered skirt that had once belonged to Gloria. He had been at the front, checking the bags for bombs and weapons. It was a joke, really, peering between the lipsticks and condoms and paper hankies. By the time she came out, at the end of the concert, dressed in her usual clothes, with Gloria's skirt in a Tesco bag, everyone had gone home. There was only the sound of the wind and the pre-Christmas traffic toiling back from the West End. Luka was there, sitting on a concrete bollard, waiting. Kirsty asked him if he'd found anything suspicious in the bags and he said only a small landmine. It hadn't seemed worth making a fuss about it, he said, spoiling everyone's evening. 'It was a good concert, though,' he said. 'I liked it.' She asked him what he liked about it and he smiled.

He had come all the way from Croatia to London, leaving his mother alone in Zagreb. His family had seen worse things than ever turned up in bags at London concerts. Kirsty felt – although Luka wasn't, ultimately, or even in the short term, her responsibility – that rejecting him was a breach of hospitality. There were no words she could say – none that were safe – to make him himself again, though she knew what they were, the unsafe ones.

7

A week after Easter, Paula rang Vivienne at work. 'Have you had a think about the "Our Families" DVD, darling? Glen needs to firm up on the numbers.'

'No, not yet. I haven't had a chance to talk to Richard,' Vivienne said. She and Paula had already had the same interchange when Vivienne had rung up to thank Paula for the party. Their conversations often had an overlapping effect, which was sometimes soothing, sometimes irritating. Vivienne preferred to be left alone at work. Then the days – working and non-working – separated themselves out, or at least blurred within their different categories. Through the glass screen of her office, Vivienne could see into the showroom. A red-headed woman, wearing a tightly belted mac, was walking aimlessly in and out of the screened compartments. The baths, basins, bidets and toilets were arranged in their style/range groups, as if they were in real bathrooms with half-walls round them. The gleaming white was sepulchral and generally calming. The groups were, in their way, like impeccable families: clean, matching, durable and with clearly defined roles. 'I don't think we're suitable,' she said, deciding she must take a unilateral decision. Her earlier excuse jarred.

'Whatever do you mean?' Paula said.

'Not perfect. As a family.'

'Darling, you're all scrummy. Who mentioned perfect? This is "*Our*". It's meant to be an inspiration to the couples who want to get married in St Dunstan's or bring their babies for baptism.'

'Richard and I aren't really screen types. I'd be hopeless.'

'Sweetie, we're not talking Hollywood,' Paula said.

Vivienne felt affronted – which was absurd. She transferred the receiver to the other ear and crashed it against her earring.

Paula was saying, 'I do think family values should be *celebrated*. Oh, before I forget, I found a pair of spotty socks in the garden. I wondered if they belonged to Martha, I know she's always stripping off.'

'Yes, they'll be hers. Don't send them. I'll pick them up some time,' Vivienne said.

'How's Richard?' Paula asked.

Vivienne hesitated, wondering whether Paula had picked up on Richard's behaviour at the lunch party: his solitary time in the garden; his failure to appear for the Pattersons' party medley. She had hoped Paula hadn't noticed.

'We were a teeny bit worried about him. He didn't seem quite on bouncy form,' Paula said.

'He could have done with more time off over Easter – but he's all right, I think.'

'You two should get away,' Paula said.

'We might do something for my mother's seventieth in June.'

'That's ages away. In any case, I was thinking more of a twosome. You know, darling, Hartley and I would always have your girls for a night, if we're free.' She broke off and made a sound as if she were licking a spoon. 'We're off on a spoiling holiday in Normandy, eating tons of cream, did I tell you? Just a few days. I might have to miss Prayer Clinic. You'll lead the meeting if I'm not back, won't you, June the third?

'That's not your ma's birthday, is it? The meeting will be at Hilly's house but she refuses point-blank to lead.'

Jake, the salesperson, was taking a very long coffee break.

Vivienne craned her neck to see if she could get a glimpse of him in the small backyard, where he went to make calls on his mobile and to smoke a cigarette. Sometimes she had the impression that Paula was keeping her up to the mark in her marriage – setting encouraging goals, as she did with church activities. Then the idea seemed far-fetched; a sign of her own insecurity – the fear that she would never pass, as people used to say, with flying colours. Jake was standing with his back to her, apparently gazing at the ventilation brick in the wall opposite. The top of a comb stuck out of the back pocket of his trousers. He had been taking longer and longer breaks, ever since she had wondered whether she should talk to him about the gospel message. 'Keep it short,' Glen had recommended. 'It can be useful to begin with a scriptural sentence that means a lot to you. Don't mention sin in your opening pitch.' But she hadn't yet said a single *word*. Jake seemed to sense that she was revving up to it. Really, she was completely useless.

'Darling, are you still there?' Paula asked.

'Yes, of course.'

'You went very quiet. But you are a quiet person. Restful. You don't rabbit on, like me.'

'Whereabouts are you going?' Vivienne said.

'Do you know Normandy?'

'No, not really.'

'Just imagine a half-timbered building in the middle of a field of cows. I'm hopeless at geography. I go somewhere and *enjoy* it and come back again.'

The woman wearing the tightly belted mac was contemplating an oval basin on a twisted pedestal that was part of the Petrarch range. She ran her hand along its curved underside. The mild sensuousness of the gesture unsettled Vivienne. Her body, slight as it was, felt surplus. She wondered which had come first, the useless feeling of her flesh or Richard's tired lack of interest. She felt ashamed, somehow, that such private things were visible, or could be heard in the voice – by Paula, at least. The red-headed woman seemed to sense she was being watched and removed her hand quickly, as if she were in a museum and feared a custodian might bear down on her for touching the sculptures. It occurred to Vivienne that if other people had noticed that Richard seemed unwell she would be justified in delving around in the study at home, checking the file where they kept the health insurance policy and having a quick look in Richard's desk. It was nothing to be ashamed of, because illness was morally neutral, unlike adultery, and didn't impugn the investigator of it with jealousy or anything dubious. All the same, she knew in advance that she would feel uncomfortable about looking. She took a deep breath. 'Paula, why did you ask about Richard? Did he say something was the matter?' she asked.

'No. He didn't say anything.' Paula paused encouragingly. As Vivienne said nothing, she continued, 'Actually, I thought he was his usual sweet self. It was Bellsie who said he seemed below par. When she went downstairs to find her bag he was, allegedly, slumped over the kitchen table.'

'He'd probably had a bit too much to drink. He'd been sober all Lent,' Vivienne said.

'Probably, darling. I wouldn't worry about it. Richard's gorgeous. In my book, he can do no wrong. "Slumped" was over the top, I'm sure. You know Bellsie. She has her own vocabulary. You're not worrying, are you?'

'No. Look, Paula, I'll have to go. I'm on my own here.' Jake was still in the yard. It wasn't a lie.

'Go, go, go. You did say "yes" to Prayer Clinic, didn't you? Put it in the diary. Thank you, angel. Lots of love. 'Bye.'

For the rest of the working day, Vivienne made an effort to suppress thoughts of Richard's malaise but business was flat and the image of Paula's guests wandering into the kitchen and gazing at her husband kept cropping up. In the late afternoon, Jake sold three bathrooms. Vivienne was glad of some action. She worked out a favourable deal for the client and sorted out the paperwork. After she had telephoned the order through, she went out to the local patisserie and bought Jake a chocolate éclair. He looked a bit nervous as he accepted the little tissue paper package tied up with blue ribbon. He was a tall, good-looking lad, with a line in flamboyant ties and a diamond chip in his ear. Nervousness didn't suit him. Vivienne said he could go home early if he wanted to. He thanked her and smiled. She hoped that if she banished the thought of witness in the workplace, eventually they would be on easy terms again. He was a promising young salesman and she didn't want to lose him.

Vivienne arrived home at seven o'clock. As she walked into the hall, she could hear the noise of dice being shaken in a pot and counters placed in plodding sequence on a board, through the open door of the kitchen. Otherwise it was a silence of meticulous cooperation. Henka, the girl who came in to look after Bethany and Martha, had a tranquillising effect on them. She had introduced them to old-fashioned games – Ludo, Snakes and Ladders, dominoes – and endlessly played with them. Vivienne thought it was all rather repetitive. Henka's main drawback was that she couldn't drive and was therefore unable to take the girls to their activities. Ability to drive had been part of the person specification for the job but Henka had scored on the point of church attendance. She was Roman Catholic, which was understandable, since she was Polish. She had stuck with her childhood faith. Vivienne went into the kitchen to say hello but Bethany and Martha were too absorbed in the game to give her more than passing kisses.

Vivienne walked across to the study and, having unfastened the security locks, pushed the window open because the room seemed airless. The Epworth paperwork was all organised in box files on open shelves. Vivienne took down the health file and flicked through the contents. She found nothing, just the policy itself, various advice notices of increases in the premiums and some old correspondence about a mole Bethany had had removed from her arm. She returned it to its place.

The desk was Richard's. It was the old-fashioned sort, made of oak, with a pull-down front and compartments inside. There was no key, so it wasn't private, just exclusively his, as the dressing table in their bedroom was hers. All couples had pieces of furniture that were particular to one or the other and, in the very old, this extended to chairs. She and Richard were too young to have special chairs, but the thought was comforting that one day this might be the case. Vivienne half wished they had reached that point. She lowered the desktop and looked inside. Richard wasn't a hoarder of memorabilia. He kept his bank statements and investments bumf for three years, then put the papers through the shredder. The only personal item was a worn leather wallet in which he kept spare credit cards, his driver's licence and a couple of baby photos of the girls. That was all. His mother was the keeper of his childhood: photographs, school reports, the weekly letters from boarding school. Not having lived with any other men apart from her father, who had also been economical with his possessions, Vivienne assumed that salting stuff away was more a female habit. The exception to the rule was business cards. There was a stack of them in one of the desk compartments. They accumulated like offerings of bread for overfed birds. Vivienne took them out and riffled through them but found nothing medical among them. She picked up the wallet. A card was sticking from one of the pockets. She wondered why it was there, in this special place, and not part of the stack. She pulled it out. It had a design on one side – a feather – and, turning it over, she saw there was a telephone number, handwritten, on the back. The style was different from a normal business card. It couldn't have come from a shop or a gallery as there was no trading name or address.

Through the open window Vivienne could hear next door's children playing table tennis in their garage – the rapid plop of bats on the ball and shouted score keeping. The boys were a few years older than Bethany and Martha, though that didn't stop the girls speaking disparagingly of them in deliberately audible voices. Their daddy had recently gone to live with another woman, taking his car with him, which was why one half of the double garage was free for the table tennis. Of course, table tennis was no substitute for a father but the boys seemed to enjoy it. Vivienne imagined the daddy returning and driving smack into the table. People couldn't expect things to stay the same.

She looked at the card again; the feather was pretty, a nice design. She went to the desk and put it back where she had found it. Then she relocked the window. The sky, striped with dark cloud, was still disconcertingly light – the debilitated light of early evening when the clocks have gone on but spring hasn't caught up – enough to give definition to the roofs in the distance. There was something depressing about the early weeks of daylight saving, Vivienne thought, parsimonious. But daylight couldn't be shifted about like money between accounts. It got its revenge by producing evenings that were dull and pale – often until the end of May, by which time the concept of saving light was irrelevant.

8

In his last week of employment Abe took a day off. He had a lie-in, then he went by tube to Liverpool Street. He would have called the office and said he was sick but illness, in the health insurance business, was a commodity. If you weren't careful you were fast-tracked to the Personal Advisory team. 'Good morning, this is Danielle speaking, could you give me your policy number, please.' 'Piss off, this is Abe and I've got the flu.' Abe had some leave owing and he had *genuinely* taken a day off work. He was proud of that. He was heading for Karumi, the sports injury treatment centre in Shoreditch, where his friend Shane worked as a receptionist. Shane was still planning to lease Japanese exercise equipment to gyms and health clubs. Abe had called him and they had arranged a time to go and look at the machinery.

Bishopsgate was the only street Abe knew where everyone kept up. They put one foot in front of the other and moved. As soon as he stepped off the escalator, people carved him up, whooshing by him as if they were on wheels, shouting at each other across him. Abe liked the part of London around Liverpool Street. He liked the reverberations between the massive Victorian buildings and the glassier buildings put up yesterday – and the way everyone, scurrying at ground level, male and female, wore Thatcher-style suits with square-cut shoulders. As it was a day off, Abe was wearing jeans and his white hooded jacket. Also his hat as there was a bit of a wind.

Abe turned off the main road and followed a tall brick wall, stylishly blackened by old pollution, then, when that came to a dead end, because the railway had right of way, he chose a side street at random and cut through an alley, dodging a stream of water that bubbled up through the concrete from a leaking pipe. He hoped he was heading in the right direction. After crossing two intersections he paused. On the far side of the road was a row comprising a half-demolished building, a betting shop, a funeral director, a sandwich bar called Vasco's. These were the first signs of commercial life since he had left Bishopsgate. Abe needed some coffee. He waited for a gap between the cars and went across.

Glancing in through the window of T. Shipley & Son, Funeral Directors, he noticed a framed poem, propped like a photograph, next to the urn. Before Neil died, funeral directors' premises seemed like gaps in the high street. Now Abe was slightly fascinated – aware that there were quirky differences between them. Unobtrusiveness came in various styles. He pressed his face against the glass to read the poem. The gist of it was that death was nothing at all and that the dead person had just gone into another room. Abe read it a second time and still couldn't make sense of it. He thought about calling in and telling whoever was in charge that they were eroding the customer base. Why not just shut up shop and reopen as a deli or a launderette? Looking beyond the window display, he saw a vase of stiff white flowers standing on a table and, just behind it, a panelled door. He supposed it must lead to a room. He tried to imagine it and summoned up an interior, closed like a box, unlit and unfurnished – but the picture lasted less than a second. He saw the reflections of the street again, a post van going past, himself staring at the glass. He thought of the cinema screen blanking out at the moment of a death. You feel the pitch into nothingness – then the credits appear and you shuffle out of your seat, assuming that's how it will always be; with the capacity to see and to stand up after the shock has worn off. Then Abe thought about Neil and felt sad and guilty, because his death had been, in a way, nothing at all.

Abe turned away and pushed open the door of Vasco's, hunching his shoulders because the doorway was narrow, as was the interior, with its seating crammed into a sliver of space along the wall. He walked past the counter – the mounds of flaked tuna, sliced tomato, chopped egg, shredded lettuce, each in plastic containers behind curved glass. There were only three customers: two women giggling over some photos on a phone and an elderly man eating a doughnut. Abe negotiated the bolted-down tables and slipped into a seat at the far end, also bolted down. He had set aside the day to replan his life. Vasco's wasn't the ideal setting but it would do for the time being. The man behind the sandwich counter was watching him. A kind-looking man with a grey moustache. Abe held up his index finger with his thumb an inch below it, to indicate that he would like an espresso. The man smiled and nodded. Abe liked an old-style sandwich bar. He even liked the sandwiches once in a while. White sliced bread, brown sliced bread, white sticks, chewy as old slippers. There was one with a breaded escalope of meat – chicken or veal – slapped inside a white stick. The smear of bright yellow butter got stuck to the breadcrumbs and the filling fell out as soon as you bit into it. He might order one of those later, if they had one. But this was the moment for creativity. He had purposely left his laptop at home. Abe fished around one-handedly in his bag and took out a clean A4 notebook. He opened it at the first page and stared at it from a wide angle, leaning against the back of the seat, as if he were long-sighted. Running the middle finger of his left hand slowly down the spiral binding of the notebook from top to bottom produced a tingly feeling that started in his fingertip and moved up through his hand and past his wrist. After a while the sensation dulled. Abe wrote 'Business Plan' at the top of the page.

'Is ready.' The man with the grey moustache was leaning over the end of the counter holding a cup of espresso.

Abe stretched up for it and said 'Cheers'. There were two paper wraps of sugar in the saucer. 'Have you got any real sugar?' he asked. The man looked puzzled. Abe mimed dipping a lump of sugar into his coffee and sucking it. The man nodded, suddenly happy, and turned to the shelf behind him. He opened a biscuit tin and handed over two small macaroons.

'Thank you,' Abe said. 'You're a star.'

The man beamed and continued his drying-up. Abe took one of the biscuits, dipped it in the coffee and sucked it. The almond taste was bitter. Abe took a swig of coffee.

'You study?' Vasco said.

'Soon. I'm going to give up work.'

The man laughed. 'What your boss say?'

'He's a tosser,' Abe said. He looked again at the title he had written. 'Business Plan'. A rational head which, following the pattern of his old school essays, would acquire a short, wind-filled, ruptured body. As the rush from the coffee hit his brain, he tore off the sheet and crumpled it into a ball.

Suddenly the café was full of people. A queue was forming at the counter for lunchtime sandwiches. Office workers started pushing for places at the tiny tables – colliding with an opposite stream who were trying to leave with their takeaways. The man with the grey moustache was working at speed, delving into the fillers and pressing them into the bread, juggling cups under the sputtering spouts of the coffee machine. He looked as if he had six hands. A chubby woman wearing a bobble hat and a tatty raincoat wedged herself into the place opposite Abe. She placed her tray, with its plate of egg sandwiches, mug of tea and iced bun, on top of Abe's notebook. Picking up one of the sandwiches, she squinted at it, before taking a bite that left a row of tooth marks in a jagged crescent moon shape. Her lower arms were covered in a fine dust of hair; the sleeves of the coat halfway between her wrists and her elbows. Abe eased his notebook out from under the tray and the white pages reappeared streaked with a film of reddish grease. In this part of the world, this district of suits, Abe's pull-on hat had given the wrong signals. Like to like, the lady must have thought. Abe ripped the stained pages out. The woman started on the iced bun. She looked at Abe over its gluey top with tired eyes. He picked up his bag and his notebook, and shimmied through the gap between the table and the end of the counter. The man with the grey moustache was strewing salami across three open baguettes as if he were dealing a pack of cards. Abe left the right money and pushed his way to the exit.

'You've forgot your studies,' the man called out as Abe passed through the door.

'No worries,' Abe said.

'Study well,' the man added – laughing at him.

Abe set off up the street to look for Karumi. The buildings he passed were uncared for, bypassed by developers; similar to the battered row of shops that Vasco's was part of and made of the same Victorian brick, the rusty colour of faded theatre curtains. The next block consisted of tall commercial properties with twice as many storeys. These frontages were boarded by black-painted panels at ground-floor level; the warehouse windows above were covered with mesh. Abe pushed open a door and entered a hallway with unplastered walls. To the left was an old-fashioned lift with a concertina gate. The stairs were enclosed in a metal cage towards the back of the building. Abe passed through the gap in the grille and started to climb. The steps resounded as if they were hollow and Abe pounded up, two at a time, glancing down into the well at each platform where the stairs turned. Every level had a door and a keypad for entry but there was no signage to indicate which businesses occupied the premises. As Abe reached the last bend, the door at the top started buzzing. He jumped the final steps and pushed it open.

The room he entered was high-ceilinged, peaceful like a courtyard, with the grey daylight filtered through paper blinds. A shallow stone bowl full of water stood in the centre with two long leather sofas to either side. A man was sitting on one of them, prodding at an electronic diary with the point of a pencil.

Shane was at the far end behind a slate-topped table. He smiled as Abe walked towards him. 'I saw you in the CCTV, coming up the stairs,' he said.

'Erase it later,' Abe said. 'When can you get away?'

'Afternoon. Threeish. Lunch is the busiest time.' Shane looked slightly puzzled.

Abe stared at the plain but beautiful objects in the show-case beside the table – bowls and black Japanese teapots. The polished wood at the back of the cabinet mirrored them, turning them to the colour of clear honey.

'Nice space to work in. Quiet,' Abe said. 'Just the water glugging and the voices.'

'Buddhist monks on a continuous loop. They're there to disguise the clicks of the credit card machine,' Shane said.

'So there's money here,' Abe said.

'Yeah, plenty. We don't get to see any of it.'

'My mum likes this sort of thing,' Abe said, referring to the chanting.

Shane bounced his head from left to right and back again. He changed the pattern of the nodding and stuck his chin in the air, as if new higher notes were resounding inside his skull. Abe laughed.

'Why *are* you here?' Shane asked.

'We're going to see your mate about the machines,' Abe said.

'Oh shit.' Shane stood up, agitated. 'We were going to do that, weren't we? I forgot to call him.' He picked up his phone and started scrolling through the options. 'He won't be around. He lives in Dorset. But there's a place over at Barking where you can go and have a look at the equipment.

Do you want the number? See if anyone's there? Sometimes there is.'

'No. It's all right,' Abe said. 'Sit down.'

Shane sat down but carried on flicking through the phone's address book.

'Aren't there any pictures?' Abe asked.

'Of the machines?'

Abe pointed at the high bare walls. 'No. Pictures of bones. I thought this was a sports injury centre.'

'People don't want to see that kind of stuff.'

'The bones are in a different room,' Abe said in a spooky voice.

Shane blinked.

'Don't worry about it,' Abe said.

'It's great you came.'

'I might go to the pub,' Abe said.

'Go on. I'll join you later. The Peacock. Not the Friendly Camel.'

'All right.' Abe left the clinic and went down the six flights of stairs and out into the street.

Abe retraced his steps; back to Vasco's, across the street, down the alley. Everything looked drab. Bishopsgate, when he got there, was no more than a thoroughfare of heavy wheeled lorries and buses, rumbling up and down. Neither the 1880s nor the 1980s cast a historical glow. Abe had noticed before the distorting effect of his mood. Which was the right way of looking? He was conscious of drilling – the persistent demolition of buildings and road stone. It set his teeth on edge; communal teeth that shook all around him, rooted in concrete. He had achieved nothing; neither the master plan nor the new career. He had been thinking for so long about quitting work, just thinking, daydreaming, really. It felt weird that he had intervened and was making it happen. Like meddling, even though it was his own life. Already the decision seemed botched somehow. Not as risky as he had thought it would be. He liked risky better than botched, he thought. One was an assessment of a situation before and the other afterwards. How had he managed to get to botched already? He was sorry that Shane's man was out of town, but he didn't take it personally. He didn't blame Shane. Abe kept walking. The weather brightened up and he pulled off his hat. He walked westwards, through Moorgate, Holborn, the West End, Bayswater. By the time he reached the slicked-up streets of Notting Hill Gate the sun was out and he had forgotten his disappointment. That was the good thing about walking. Somewhere along the way he had missed the Peacock.

Three

1

The high street of Harrow-on-the-Hill was full of returning boys and the traffic at a standstill. Richard had failed to take account of the new summer term. He put his arm across the back of the passenger seat and looked out of the rear window. Another car was already behind, tight on his bumper. The woman at the wheel smiled complacently. Bethany caught Richard's eye. 'How did we get in this mess?' she asked.

'We were moving. Then everything stopped,' Richard said.

'Stop bloody hooting!' Bethany shouted to the car next to them. 'You're giving me a headache.'

'Quiet, please,' Richard said.

In the wing mirror, Richard could see Martha put her hands over her shoulders and pull at the two ends of a silk scarf that Frances had lent her. 'Jacquard,' Frances had said it was. Martha had liked the word. Her face was nearly hidden. She caught her breath as the cloth pressed against her windpipe.

'Careful, Martha,' Richard warned.

Richard glimpsed his younger daughter, lifting her face in the direction of the mirror, examining individual strands of loose hair against the light and tucking them into the scarf.

Everyone was beeping, for no known reason – more for general jollity. The sun was out for the first time in weeks and the colours were as clear as the Japanese paper flowers the girls floated in water. Cars were parked and double parked, and parents clung on to their vehicles as if fastened to outcrops on a rock face. They obstructed the road. Boys carelessly left the grown-ups and formed in groups. 'Goodbye, George.' 'Goodbye Ollie.' 'We can't leave the car, darling.' The boys weren't interested in saying goodbye. Traffic from the right was now looping round in front of Richard's car. People carriers nudged up close, their windscreens like menacing, oversized spectacles. The beeping carried on, expressing nothing more than stupidity past a certain point. Richard and his daughters waited as if they had suddenly become good at waiting – turned in on themselves – listening to the regular cheeps of Martha sucking her thumb. Eventually a key player shifted and the vehicles started to move.

Richard steered round the obstacles and wound a path down the hill, past an unbroken line of parked cars. He turned into the tennis club car park and found a space at the far end of the tarmac. 'We've made it, girls,' he said.

He accompanied Bethany and Martha to the changing pavilion, then walked back to the road. He had forgotten that tennis was starting up again. Vivienne had had to remind him. There it was on the noticeboard; Saturday mornings at nine o'clock. Richard had felt unable to refuse to chauffeur the girls, on the grounds that tennis was in Harrow. It had seemed ridiculous to make an excuse. He had made a simple resolution to keep away from Abe's road. That, he hoped, would do the trick.

Richard turned to look through the chicken wire fence at the children lining up, his own two among them. The air shone. Even the shadows were bright. Another summer beginning, he thought. He was bothered by the 'having to make the most of' that didn't colour the other seasons. 'Hang on,' he wanted to say. 'I'm not ready for this.' Other people seemed not to be affected, certainly not his daughters. They simply enjoyed themselves, full of high spirits to be out of doors with their arms and legs bare. His own dark-blue shirt seemed unseasonal. He rolled up the sleeves, turning the cloth over and over and exposing his pale forearms. The girls appeared tiny in the distance across three tennis courts. They were too far away for them to see him wave unless they were watching out for him – little figures wearing shorts and T-shirts and white tennis shoes, sunhats, too, because the day would be hot. Richard waved all the same, before turning away. He walked up the hill to the high street and went into a café.

The long room was crowded; heavy with the fatty smell of reheated croissants. At first there appeared to be no boundaries between the people who occupied the space, nor between their furious talking, but as Richard wandered around trying to find a spare seat, his eyes separated out groups who were more or less facing each other across coffee cups and plates of scattered crumbs. He found a way between them, stepping over the bulky feet of sprawling, overgrown boys, and made for an alcove off the main room into which two tiny tables had been squashed. A couple occupied one but the other was free. Richard lowered his head, brushed aside some overhanging greenery and sat down on a small iron chair. The noise in the bower was less strident. He pulled out his newspaper and opened it at the point he had stopped reading at breakfast, folding back the pages until they made a neat rectangle. As he flattened the newspaper on the table, he noticed the woman across to his right, staring into her empty coffee cup, stabbing her teaspoon into it as if she were stubbing out a cigarette. His eyes were drawn to the gesture and the force that the woman put into it.

'I tried not to call you,' she said.

Her companion said nothing.

'I tried. But ... it didn't work.' The grinding on the bottom of the coffee cup began again.

The man remained silent.

'It's been difficult,' she said. 'I didn't know what to do.'

Out of the corner of his eye, Richard saw the man lean

across the table and reach for the spoon. He took it from the woman's slim fingers with his larger ones and laid it in the saucer.

'I needed to see you,' the woman said. 'Not to do anything. Just to see you – to ground this whole thing.' She hesitated. She was swilling the dregs of coffee around in her cup as if it were good claret. 'Three weeks ago. I managed three weeks.'

A girl wearing a checked waistcoat and a full-length apron entered the alcove. 'Would you like another of those?' she asked.

'No,' the man said. 'Thank you,' he added. The girl had already turned to Richard. She was standing over him, pulling on a piece of hair that covered one eye.

'I'll have a cappuccino, please,' Richard said.

'Any food? Panini with char-grilled peppers, spring rolls in lemon dip, couscous salad, mini pizza selection.'

'No, thanks,' Richard said. 'Just coffee.'

The girl walked away. The arrangement of the short skirt showing in the inverted V of the apron made her look oddly geriatric, as if she had forgotten to pull down her dress after using the toilet. Richard's neighbours had fallen silent. The woman kept looking at the man. Her eyes weren't steady; it was as if fast-moving clouds passed across them. Richard was disturbed to be sitting so close – a non-participating third in this exchange, which was somehow inappropriate for the time of day. Seduction was turned inside out, showing the way it had been stitched together and the crude form of construction. Richard was alarmed by the woman's intensity, the negative energy that she sent in gusts across the table. It affected him, who was nothing to do with the situation. He wondered, since it was the beginning of term, whether the couple were parents of different returning boys. They were the right sort of age. But he didn't like to speculate on other people's personal business; it made him uncomfortable, as if conjecture was participating in a lie. He wished the girl with the apron would return. When his coffee arrived he drank it too quickly, scalding his mouth.

Richard left the café, leaving the correct money on the table. He walked along the high street towards the churchyard, drawn to the shadows which, from a distance, appeared green, underneath the canopy of new leaves. He thought of Bethany and Martha – what complications of relationship they might get caught in. He longed for them to be happy. Bethany would remain bold, he hoped, able to say what she wanted. He and Vivienne weren't always good at that. And Martha? He smiled, remembering her in her usual state of undress, tearing across Paula's lawn on Easter Day.

Once inside the churchyard, Richard went along the footpaths, careful of the uneven ground. Some of the old graves pushed the earth up and some fell into it, taking the lie of the path with them. There were too many trees and tombs, too many secret corners, to achieve a clear line of vision, but Richard sensed that the place was empty of boys and parents, visitors of any kind. A gardener was tidying up, only just visible, camouflaged by the leaf shadow pattern on his back. He was using a broom and a hoe, setting them aside every now and then to bend and tug at a misplaced weed or root with his bare hands. He would be there again next day, or next week, to pull up the replacements. Richard skirted round the man, envying the diligence and the repetitive actions. He trod cautiously, though the gardener was too absorbed to notice him. Richard went into the church porch and unlatched the door. The smell of old stone and old books seeped out as he edged the door open. Once inside, he had to put weight against the heavy wood to heave it shut.

The church was pleasantly cool. Richard crossed the aisle and sat down in a pew. He checked his watch. Half an hour remained before he had to return to the tennis courts. He felt secure here, out of the way. He wasn't going to pray. Praying was the wrong activity, a lonely occupation – too agitating without the presence of other praying people – not just stirring up thoughts of his own that were better left undisturbed but spoiling this Saturday peace. He wanted peace. If he asked God for help, he would need to bring to mind why he needed it and then he'd be back on the compulsive journey that looped back on itself. He sat silently, closed off from within and without, as if underwater.

There were voices outside in the porch. A man talking, perhaps addressing the gardener. Reluctantly, Richard stood up, brushed his knees from habit and walked to the end of the pew. He went towards the north door, which wasn't in use, and examined the memorial to its left – a woman lying draped over a tomb, her head concealed, some curled locks of hair escaping over her left arm. Richard bent and looked at the words carved beneath to find out who she was. *John Henry North*, he read, *Judge of the Admiralty – Ireland. Honoured, Revered, Admired, Beloved, Deplored by the Irish Bar, the Senate and his County.* The text continued at some length. For a second Richard was taken aback to read a man's name. Then he remembered the displacement, common in tombs and memorials; the depiction, not of the deceased, but of grief itself – or the grieving spouse. The dead had the script, the bereft were dumb.

Richard himself had been dumb at the crematorium in Essex where Jamie's funeral had taken place. He hadn't opened his mouth. There had been no hymns and no communal prayers – nothing to join in with. Music was played on the sound system and strangers got up to speak. The chapel had been packed. People were crammed into the pews and others, including Richard himself, were standing at the back. The family, dressed in black party clothes, had occupied the front, no doubt with Jamie's half-sisters among them. Richard had no way of knowing who was who and had been too stunned to start guessing. At the end of the service the doors had been opened by an attendant and Richard had gone outside before the traditional peeling off from the front began. He stepped off the tarmac where the cars of the next funeral were waiting, on to a wide gravel path. The air was still damp from an early-morning downpour. There was a metal gate at the far end of the path, flanked by conifers, and he kept walking towards it through pools of water that hadn't yet drained away. The printed service sheet was in his pocket. He had no recall of what was written on it. Neither music nor words were what had bound him and Jamie together. 'Are you asleep?' Richard used to say in the night, having dozed and woken. 'Not any more,' Jamie replied. The quietest part of the night was the best for Richard. Then he forgot himself. He was frightened by what had bound him to Jamie and by its vanishing.

Somewhere, on the way back to London from Essex, Richard lost the printed sheet – of all things to lose. He couldn't understand what had happened to it. He had shown his ticket on the train, bought another ticket for the tube, let himself in with his door key. He had gone through his pockets again and again. His feet were sopping wet.

The door on the other side of the church creaked open. The sunlight came in, making a path that extended beyond where Richard was standing; a tapering wedge of bright dust. He heard footsteps, habituated and purposeful, going towards the east end of the church. He waited until they were safely away, then he turned and made for the exit.

Setting off back down the hill to the car, Richard took the same route that he had taken to come up, only in reverse; that is, avoiding Abe's road. The houses he passed were large, red-brick, tile-hung, with complicated chimneys and excrescences. The plots around them were deep and the tall trees, as old as the buildings, hid the smaller houses that lay behind. Possibly, in winter, odd rooftop shapes emerged between the branches, but at this time of year new leaves were growing, expanding by the hour, filling the gaps. The proximity of the next road only a hundred or so metres away – and the fact that this was the end of Richard's Saturday excursion, not the beginning – caused a kind of diffused anguish in him, which grew worse with every step.

Richard remembered every detail of Abe's house. He was still preoccupied by having discovered it. An address was almost as impersonal as a telephone number but a house that he had stood in front of, and could call to mind, had substance. Seeing the cottage with the blue door and the broken gate had been, in an odd way, like meeting Abe for a second time. He could place him. Richard had to admit that he had been reassured by the look of the exterior, its innate respectability. There had been moments since January when he had wondered whom exactly he had brought home with him. He was in no doubt of the wrongness of what he had done, but he had been troubled also by a lack of judgement of another kind and of the risk he had taken.

Richard guessed that the couple in the café had known each other for a while – longer than a night. No one would make such heavy weather of a single night. On the scale between fantasy and reality, it was hard to know where to place such a small unit of time. Richard put it nearer fantasy but he wasn't certain. He tried not to think of Abe. People fell over themselves to help you improve your memory, prepared to sell you books, lectures, vitamins, sticky notes, gingko biloba. There was the man in the ad who would teach you to remember if you sent him a cheque. The pen-and-ink sketch of his face had appeared in the newspapers, unchanged, since Richard's childhood. But forgetting was just as much of an art. Richard wished, for present use, that he had retained more knowledge of the period following Jamie's death – that he had paid more attention to the signs of recovery along the way. He imagined that, had he kept some sort of diary, progress would have appeared in the entries – in the words themselves – showing how, on given dates, he had re-entered the everyday world. But there was no diary. He hadn't had the concentration to write and besides, the idea of fixing those weeks would have been hateful to him.

Richard's awareness of his surroundings and of the fine weather had gone. The strengthening heat was making him tense. He took his handkerchief out of his trouser pocket and rubbed it over his face. In his mind he was going down a parallel road. In this case, literally, the parallel road, and imagining he was on it, telling himself that he could have been on it and might as well be there. He walked more and more slowly, like a machine winding down, and eventually came to a halt. A dog in a nearby house started yapping and jumping up at the window, maddened by the stranger who lingered by his territory. The yapping became more frantic and the dog hurled itself at the glass. Richard started walking again, back up the hill. He seemed to be heading all the way to the top. But there was an unmade-up lane to the right which cut through to the next street. Richard took it and emerged in Abe's road.

2

Laura McDermott had got up early to teach violin. Her first pupil on Saturday arrived at eight thirty and from then on she packed them in at half-hourly intervals until one o'clock. It made for a long morning but she had her mortgage to think of. She couldn't teach nine pupils in a row without a dose of caffeine and a few drags on a cigarette, so she took a five-minute break by the back door between ten and twelve o'clock and tried to remember not to take it in the same lesson week on week. Some children were glad of a rest from her vigilance – they were told to carry on practising 'Boogie Blues' or 'Sheltering in the Wood' until her return – but others had been primed by parents to make sure they got their money's worth. 'Daddy pays you to teach me violin, not to smoke nasty cigarettes.' That was Juno Bailey. She was transferred to the eight thirty slot. Mr Bailey now delivered Juno, wearing his red towelling dressing gown. Laura spotted him in the car.

Wilfie Golding was a sweetie. He was six and wanted her to be happy. He brought her presents – a pigeon feather or a picture he'd painted – and commented on her bracelets. When she had a child she wanted him to be like Wilfie Golding. She knew that if she suggested that he shared her break with her, Wilfie would be only too glad to fall in with the idea. He would sit on the back step while she sipped her coffee and he would never, ever, tell on her, even if they wasted the entire lesson. However, she had standards and wouldn't take advantage of his good nature. She left him struggling with 'Boogie Blues' or 'Sheltering in the Wood', the same as the others, and he didn't sputter to a stop in her absence, because he had a sense of rhythm and remembered to count.

She could hear him in the front room. 'Ta ta tata ta, ta tata TAA,' she sang from the kitchen. Then she leant forward and lit her cigarette from the gas jet under the coffee pot, before turning off the heat and pouring the coffee into a mug. The back door was already open, waiting for her. She sat on the step, hitching up her skirt so that the sun warmed her legs. She rang her boyfriend on her mobile but he was still in bed, half asleep. She told him she would call back later.

Wilfie was persevering. He was playing all the repeats and had gone for a reprise. When she returned to the front room, Laura was surprised to see that he had moved away from the music stand and was standing with his back to her, bowing away, up and down, and craning his head to look out of the window.

'Mind the cat, Wilfie,' she said. 'You're about to knock into it. Stop at the G. Ta tata TAA. Good.'

'He's gone now,' Wilfie said.

'Who's gone?' she asked.

Wilfie shrugged his shoulders. 'A man,' he said. He went back to the music stand. Laura picked up her violin.

At the end of the lesson Laura took Wilfie out to the car where his mum was waiting. 'He's doing fine,' she said, as Wilfie's mum leant across to let him in through the passenger door. 'He played without the copy today. 'Bye, Wilfie, see you next week.' She stood and waved as the car drove away, then went back up the path. As she was going into the house, Laura heard someone stop by the gate. She turned round. A man, wearing a dark shirt and pale jeans, was standing there. 'Can I help you?' she asked.

'Do you teach the violin?' he said.

'Yes, I do. Did someone recommend me?'

'Not exactly,' he said. 'I was passing and saw the little chap with the violin case come out of the house.'

'Wilfie.' She paused. 'Are you looking for a violin teacher?' The man had no children with him but he had the look of a father, not a prospective pupil. He was better looking, though, than most of the fathers – nice eyes.

He hesitated. 'Maybe. I have two daughters.' He was plucking at the shrub in the pot by the gate. Laura had noticed earlier in the week that it had stopped producing new shoots and was going brown at the top.

'Something's happened to that plant. It could be die-back. Is that a particular disease, do you know, or does it simply mean well on the way to dead?' she said.

He removed his hand quickly. 'I don't know.'

Laura glanced down the road. There was no sign of the silver jeep that Serge's father drove. Serge was often late. Sometimes he came without his violin. Once he came without the bow. 'Come in for a minute, if you like,' she said. The man didn't move. 'Don't, if you don't want to,' she added.

'No, I will. Thank you. If it's not too much trouble,' he said, taking a step forward, shaking fragments of dead leaf from his hands.

Laura went into the house. The man followed and shut the door behind him so quietly that she turned round to check that it hadn't been left open.

'Is it all right to shut it?' he asked.

'Of course,' she said. 'I prefer it shut.'

'The dads are usually full of themselves – on some kind of ego trip,' she said. 'It's refreshing to meet one who isn't. Really.'

The man didn't sit down. He stood on the threadbare rug, looking round the front room. He was taking everything in. The white lanterns, smothered with dust, that were strung round the mirror and only looked pretty at night, the toppling stacks of sheet music, the upright piano, the innumerable candles in varying states of hardened drip. He said nothing, but judging from his expression he seemed to think it was a fascinating place. Laura, who also remained standing, didn't launch into the usual questions: children's names, ages, signs of musical potential. She was wondering if this man was as tentative in all walks of life – in bed, for example – and how that worked out. She rolled one of the beaded bracelets from her wrist and, pulling her hair back from her face into a knot, twisted the bracelet round the clump of hair.

'I actually hate quite a few of them – the dads,' she said, twisting the bracelet tighter. 'Serge's father wanted to pay for the lessons by debit or credit card. He couldn't understand why I didn't have one of those little machines where you punch in your pin number. "Hang on," I said. "I'm not a shop or a service station. And I don't give Nectar points, either. Or air miles." That shut him up.'

The man nodded. While Laura was talking, he had glanced once or twice at the ceiling, as if wondering who was upstairs. She was finding it hard to get his full attention. 'To be honest, it didn't. Nothing shuts the dads up. That was just wishful thinking. But the kids are all right. I like kids, even if their parents have done their best to turn them into whingers. If I had a quid for every time they say they've got arm ache, I'd be as rich as they are.'

'What's the cure?' the man asked.

'Revolution. I don't know,' she said. 'This is the dark age of materialism.'

'Sorry, I meant for arm ache. I can imagine that the young ones might get a bit tired.'

'Whose side are you on?' she said. 'I tell them to lie down on the floor and close their eyes. They soon get bored. Boredom is a form of anxiety.'

'I suppose that's right, I never thought of it like that.'

Laura wanted to suggest that he lay down on the floor.

Certainly, he looked very uncomfortable standing up. She was thinking more in terms of Alexander Technique than anything more intimate, but she had a desire to put his head in her lap and stroke his hair. Maybe his forehead too, since it kept creasing up. She wondered how he'd react to the idea. He was diffident but she had a feeling he might say yes, although the floor was none too clean. She looked straight at him and for the first time he looked straight back.

'You sing, don't you?' he said.

The doorbell rang. 'That will be Serge,' she said. 'All music teachers sing – after a fashion. Stay there, I'll just go and let him in.'

Laura returned, steering the boy over to the sofa, aware that she was putting malign pressure on his plump shoulder. 'Start unpacking, Serge, and I'll tune your violin for you in a second. I'm just going to find a prospectus.'

Laura went to the piano and picked up one of the sheets on which were printed a résumé of her teaching methods together with the term dates and her charges. 'Have one of these.' She handed it to her visitor. 'Give me a call if you decide to go ahead. I'm fairly booked up but I'll see what I can do. Perhaps your girls could join the Tuesday group.'

'Thank you,' he said. He took the sheet from her. He folded it and seemed as if he was about to put it in his pocket but he checked the movement and unfolded it, looked at it again. 'Laura McDermott.'

'Yes,' she said. 'That's me.'

Serge had taken out his violin from its blue felt interior and had put it between his knees as if it were a cello. Laura had been watching him out of the corner of her eye. Now he began to grind the bow over the strings. 'Stop that, Serge,' she said.

'Is that your professional name?' the man asked.

'It's my name,' she said.

'Laura,' he said, but not addressing her, just saying the word – as if it wasn't anyone's name. He seemed perplexed.

He put the sheet in his back pocket. 'Does anyone else teach here?'

'No.'

'No one called Kirsty?'

'No,' she repeated. 'Who's Kirsty?'

He shook his head. 'I've somehow. I don't know ...' he tailed off. 'I mustn't take up any more of your time. You've been very kind.' He straightened up and put his hand out to her. 'Richard Epworth,' he said, suddenly formal. She saw flecks of grey in his hair as he leant forward.

Serge had resumed the grinding, this time with the back of the bow. Laura put her hands over her ears.

'I must go,' Richard Epworth said.

'Wise choice,' Laura said. 'I'll see you out.'

She went to the front door with him and watched as Richard Epworth went down the path and through the gate. 'Good luck,' she called out. She didn't know why.

3

Vivienne blew the film of dust that the afternoon sun had made visible on the mantelpiece. Then she picked up the out-of-date At Home invitation propped up against the wall – Paula and Hartley asking them to lunch on Easter Sunday – and tore it in half.

'Richard?' Vivienne said.

He was sitting on the sofa, tipped back, staring up at the ceiling. 'I was tired that's all. It's been a long week,' he said.

'We all have weeks,' Vivienne said.

Through the closed door of the living room Richard could hear the clucking voices of cartoon characters of a DVD the girls were watching in the kitchen. 'I know, I know, it was all my fault. I've said so. But I was only twenty minutes late. Diane Whats-her-name, the coach, was there. The girls were fine.'

Vivienne hadn't reproached him when he first returned home from the tennis courts, choosing instead to have Saturday lunch in peace. Now he understood why she had shut all the doors.

'That's the second time you've been late picking the girls up,' Vivienne said. She walked over to the waste-paper basket and dropped the two halves of the invitation into it.

'When was the first, then? Tennis has only just started,' Richard said.

'After Julian's party. I didn't say anything about tennis.'

Richard got up from the sofa and walked over to the window, nearly tripping over the stack of English holiday cottage brochures that lay on the floor.

'I'll get rid of those. I keep forgetting about them,' Vivienne said.

'It's not for another month or so, is it?'

There was no escaping Frances's seventieth-birthday weekend. Whatever good feelings Richard had had about it had dispersed. A cottage near the Cuckmere estuary in Sussex had been chosen and a deposit put down. He tried to visualise the silvery loops of the Cuckmere River snaking down to the sea, as if he were seeing it from a light aircraft or a vantage point high on the Downs. He tried not to home in on the 'Lovely cottage, sleeps six'. He thought of driving alone along the motorway – a long, grey, straight stretch between hills – and that also helped.

'The first weekend in June. You definitely can't get away on the Friday afternoon?' Vivienne said.

'No. I've already told you. I've got a dinner to go to. I'll drive down later. There'll be less traffic.'

The neighbour who lived across the road was about to cut his hedge with an electric trimmer. Wearing a baseball cap, goggles and heavy leather gauntlets, Craig looked like a dangerous gnome. He caught sight of Richard gazing out and raised his free hand. Richard responded with a nod. The motor started up and Craig began to plane the fuzzy top of the foliage with even strokes.

'Is Julian the boy who lives in that huge house at the top of the Hill?' Richard asked.

'Yes. You remember going there, don't you?'

Richard winced. 'Why didn't you talk about it then, if it bothered you? That was weeks ago. Why wait till now? That's what I can't understand about you, Vivienne.'

'I wasn't bothered.'

'Exactly.'

The soundtrack from the DVD was suddenly louder. The

girls must have turned up the volume. There was a crackle, as of explosives, and then the clatter of falling rubble. The girls burst out laughing.

'I offered to go to the garden centre. You said that there was enough lawn fertiliser in the shed left over from last year. It was just a question of finding it,' he said.

'I did say that,' she agreed.

'So there was nothing you wanted me to do. I went for a walk. It was a beautiful day. It *was* a beautiful day.' He glanced out again. Craig had started on the side of the hedge, was sweeping across it with diagonal strokes. The pavement was topped with a layer of leaves and Craig was ankle deep in them. Richard knew nothing about Craig. Only that he had a wife, Anne, twin boys and a vintage VW that was parked in the garage. Was there even the slightest chance that Craig would hang around outside a stranger's house, or, when the stranger generously and hospitably took him in, inform her that she had mistaken her own identity? He thought, on the whole, not. And John Henry North, Judge of the Admiralty, would he have done such a thing? The inscription on the monument was full, but somehow, although John North had been 'Deplored by the Irish Bar, the Senate and his County', that particular unwise choice hadn't been part of the list.

'And before Julian's party. Where were you then?' Vivienne said.

'Somewhere similar, I suppose. I can't remember.' Richard was beginning to dislike the sound of his voice.

'It's a good thing I didn't say yes to the "Our Families" DVD,' Vivienne said.

'Say that again.'

'I said, it's a good thing I didn't say yes to the "Our Families" DVD. Paula said Glen wants us to be in it.'

Richard couldn't see Vivienne's face. She was placing their used coffee cups on the tray. 'You said no?' he asked.

'No, I just didn't say yes.' She straightened up.

'That's no bloody use with Paula. Who's eligible?'

'People like us, I suppose. We're church members and we have children.'

'So Paula and Hartley don't qualify?'

'They're a couple, not a family.'

'But they're happy,' Richard said. 'Totally united, as far as one can see.' He glanced at Vivienne and saw that the remark was unwelcome. 'Not like two halves of an egg, more like a double buggy,' he continued. But Vivienne failed to respond. Richard felt the weariness in his shoulders and his head, as if effort was needed to be held in place. He knew, in that moment, where his spine might protrude and cave in when he reached old age.

'I'll tell Paula a definite no, then,' Vivienne said, her face poker calm, but her lower lip trembling in a disorganised way. 'Do you think the girls *would* wander off on their own from the tennis courts? They said they were waiting by the entrance gate. Where would they go? They're basically sensible, aren't they?' Her expression had changed, was now beseeching.

'Yes,' Richard said. 'They're basically sensible. And I did pick them up, albeit late – and useless.'

Richard took a deep breath and leant forward to gather up the pile of brochures. They would be better off without the presence of so many English cottages set against blue sky. 'Sorry, Vivienne,' he said.

4

The house in Iverdale Road absorbed as much heat from the sun as a matchwood shack – only Kirsty's basement stayed tepid. It was as if the spec builders of the 1900s had skimped on a layer of bricks – or perhaps it was the design that was at fault; the room that fitted directly under the slate roof without an intervening attic. Even with all the windows open a draught was hard to come by. What came through the gaps was noise, day and night: faulty bus brakes that shrieked like hurt animals and the repeated whoosh of passing cars. There was no breeze to cool down the local infants and stop them from wailing – nor to disperse the intermittent stench from next door's drains.

Abe thought of his father skulking about on the bottom two floors. He imagined him stooping, half asleep, under the low basement ceiling, holding a spliff between his thumb and index finger, raising it to his mouth out of vagueness rather than for pleasure. He had assumed that Neil's choice of leaving the upper floors empty had come from laziness, combined with an ignorance of property values and ways of increasing them – even from an aversion to increasing value on principle. Abe didn't credit his father with making practical decisions but he had to acknowledge, in the present heat, that maybe Neil's choice of carelessly ignoring half of the house hadn't been so stupid after all. Abe found himself thinking of his father. Since giving up full-time work, he thought of him often. He had intimations of failure – sensing what that might feel like – while anticipating that he had endless time and talent to ward failure off.

By eleven at night the air had cooled a little, but Abe left the portable electric fan running. He picked up a solitary banana from the bowl on the table and began to peel it. He had eaten the end of a loaf earlier. Now he felt hungry. He went through to his kitchen and opened one of the cupboards. There was a selection of vitamins in brown bottles, also some small jars; chilli flakes, curry powder, coriander seed, mixed herbs. He had tea, coffee, a tin of tomato puree, a packet of basmati rice. Abe shook the rice packet. Empty – like his bank account. He aimed it at the sleek Swedish bin.

Abe had started sharing the shifts at Karumi with his friend, Shane, working a few afternoons a week. The pay was fairly basic. His boss made a lot of the fact that the employees could have treatment at fifty per cent but as Abe didn't have tendonitis, sciatica, trapped nerve or any kind of back, neck or joint pain, this wasn't much of a perk. The Japanese-exercise-equipment idea, which had seemed poised like a Hokusai wave ready to break, was now more of an outgoing tide. Neither the keyholder of the storage facility in Barking, where the equipment was allegedly housed, nor the head man in Dorset returned their calls. On weekday mornings, when Kirsty struggled in to central London in the rush hour, Abe took himself off to the park. The trees, heavy with leaves, made interlocking pools of shadow down the main path and straggly roses had begun flowering in the formal beds. Abe chose a tree that stood by itself – a copper beech – and lay beneath it, catching up on the sleep that eluded him at night. The sleep was weird; not really restful. He dreamt, on one occasion, of dancing a slow sexy dance with the man who worked at the checkout of the local Costcutter. This was an unhurried, memorable dream, not spoiled by the furtive knowledge that in reality the man was charm-free. Mostly they were short napping dreams about work, being late, fighting muggers. Through half-closed eyes, Abe was aware of the park characters who sat on benches and walked between the shrubs, muttering to themselves. They left him alone in his own private shadow with his head resting on his T-shirt.

Abe finished the banana and lit a cigarette. Sometimes he thought that he would be forced back into marketing. He couldn't doze his life away. The part of his brain that was used for work had moulded to marketing ways. No one had told him how careful you had to be about your first career choice – that there might be divorce proceedings but certainly not annulment. He could write the marketing job ads in his head. There was no need to buy a newspaper and turn to the appointments. *An outstanding opportunity to make a major contribution to a growing business with a highly satisfied customer base*. He played around, shuffling words. *A growing opportunity to make a highly satisfied contribution to a major business with an outstanding customer base.* He could see the layout of the imaginary application form; the creepy section headed *Is there anything else you would like to tell us about yourself?* No, was the answer. The pages of the A4 notebook he carried around with him remained blank.

At about midnight Kirsty's doorbell rang. As the bell box was placed high in the hall, the sound carried all the way up the house. After a few seconds it went again; insistent this time, as if the person outside was leaning on the button. Abe went out to the top landing. 'Shut the fuck up,' he said. He switched on the light, leant over the banister rail and looked down the well of the house, but there was no sign of Kirsty. He came clattering down the front stairs. A pale face was pressed up against the glass of the front door. Minicab drivers were face-pressers, especially if they'd come to the wrong address. Friends generally weren't. Abe opened the door, prepared to slam it straight back. Luka was on the doorstep. 'Where is Kirsty?' he said.

'No idea,' Abe said.

'I'm homeless,' Luka said. The 'h' at the beginning of the word emerged guttural and melancholy from far down his throat.

'You'd better come in,' Abe said.

Luka stepped inside. Kirsty came along the hall just then, fresh out of the bath, making wet footprints on the floor. She stopped when she saw Luka and pulled the belt of her kimono tight round her. 'Luka. What are you doing here?' she asked.

'He's homeless,' Abe said, shutting the door.

Luka stood holding a large zip-up holdall in front of him with both hands. The bag was heavy and hung sagging a few inches from the floor but he didn't put it down. 'My house has been repossessed by the landlord's mortgage company,' he said.

'Which house?' Kirsty asked.

'My house. In New Cross. We have all had to leave.'

'It's really late, Luka,' Kirsty said.

'I'm sorry. I have been travelling all day to far parts of London, taking my boxes, my possessions, to various houses for safe keeping,' Luka said.

'Couldn't any of those people put you up – the ones you took the boxes to?' Kirsty asked.

'No. That is impossible. These are cousins of people my mother knows in Zagreb.'

Abe admired the way Luka said 'no'. The word, stripped of limp, English negativity, had real intent behind it. Luka seemed more foreign than when he had last seen him. Abe couldn't understand how that had come about. Surely the longer a person spent in a place, the more acclimatised they became? Yet Luka, having seemed like a real Londoner previously, now put up resistance to blending in. His black hair projected defiantly outwards but his body had shrunk into itself. His English was odd. He made a special pocket of air around himself that was not London air.

'What about Eugen? Can't you stay with him?' Kirsty asked.

'He has gone back to Croatia,' Luka replied, giving Abe a sidelong look of reproach.

'Oh Luka, you must be able to find somewhere else?' Kirsty said. After her initial questions she had caved in. Luka would interpret this as a 'yes'. Understandably. Abe would do the same himself.

Luka put the bag down on the floor. 'Where shall I sleep?' he asked.

'I'll leave you two to it,' Abe said.

5

A few days later Kirsty called Marlene to tell her what had happened. 'This doesn't surprise me. But you'll cope, Kirst. You always do. Have you been to New Cross to check out the story? Call Zoë or Leanne. How transparent of Luka to talk of repossession,' Marlene said. 'He could easily have used one of those legal words that has no meaning.'

Kirsty had been clear about Luka's sleeping on the sofa. *That* she hadn't been feeble about – and had got the instruction in immediately by showing him into the living room on the night he arrived and handing him the sleeping bag. He had a new job as a relief porter in a private hospital. No questions had been asked about his employment status but because the place was at the end of a long suburban lane, miles from a tube station, he had had to buy a second-hand bicycle to get to and from work. There were now two bikes in the narrow hall, Luka's and Declan's, and hardly room to get past. 'Don't you do enough wheeling with the trolleys?' Abe said. 'This place looks like a fucking bicycle shed.' Kirsty imagined Luka wearing surgeon's green scrubs – though that wasn't what porters wore – pushing bed-bound patients in and out of cavernous lifts. All week he had been asleep when Kirsty left for work in the morning. She walked past the closed door in the hall and went straight out to the street, feeling as if she were the lodger, checking out of her own guest house. When she returned in the evening the living room door was still closed, but at that time of day she opened it and went in. She wandered around, trying to maintain right of way, like a rambler following an old path along the edge of a field. She drew the living-room curtains fully and let in the light. Luka's clothes were in the zip-up bag. A pillow and a folded sleeping bag were placed on top of it in a forlorn pile.

Kirsty looked about dispassionately, as if the room were no longer hers. She remembered the rolls of the dust that used to collect in the corners and round the legs of the furniture, like dry ice blown on to a stage set. They had gone – cleaned up in an early zealous burst – together with Neil's derelict props: crockery and empty bottles used as ashtrays. But the furniture remained. Kirsty stared at the battered-looking sofa. It seemed to have aged further, used as a bed. The creases in the Indian cloth that covered it were in permanent pleats. Having been shut up for hours on end with Luka inside, the room had regained its former mustiness. She could smell that someone had slept there, but also Neil's old druggy, alcoholic smells – weed, cigarettes, Nag Champa, wine, whisky – which she had thought her housekeeping and open-windows policy had done away with for ever. The feelings Kirsty had had as a child, of being a stranger in the house, of not belonging, came back to her. She didn't feel quite at home. Picking up the indistinct sound of voices on Abe's television, coming from upstairs, she wondered if she would have recognised Neil's voice if she heard it again.

Sometimes it crossed her mind that she and Abe were there under false pretences and that someone with a better claim would ask for the property back. She imagined a man watching a CCTV screen in a faraway room, idly looking at them – not with sinister intent, but simply looking, killing time, until the moment came to pull the plug on them. Since moving in, Kirsty had received several calls on the land line from people who asked to speak to Neil. Mostly they were cold callers who wanted to inform Mr Rivers that he had won a trip to the Caribbean or to persuade him to change his telephone provider. On one occasion it had been a woman called Dido and another time a woman with an actorly voice who wouldn't give her name. Kirsty had had to tell these people that Neil had died. The conversations had left her shaky. Neither of the women she had spoken to had known that Neil had a daughter.

Kirsty went down to the basement and saw Luka through the kitchen window. He was propping up the post in the garden fence, always in the same spot of shade, bare-chested, smoking his sprouting roll-ups – looking as miserable and proud as if he were waiting to be shot for a matter of honour. Kirsty found it hard to describe to herself how she felt when she saw him there. Every evening it was the same feeling, which administered a shock, like a jolt from a recurring dream and didn't increase or lessen as the week went by. It was as if someone had planted a full-size tree which she hadn't ordered or chosen, but which she knew for certain was impossible to dig up without either killing the tree or wrecking the garden.

Kirsty had to take a deep breath before going out to join him. Having said 'hi', she picked up her small garden fork and worked in the shade cast by the shadow of the house. After being stuck in the shop all day, she liked kneeling on an old blanket and grubbing about in the flower bed she had made. The plants were only a few inches high, but they were trusting, wanting to live. Presumably they would have preferred to be somewhere else, a royal park or a sprinkled garden, but they were doing their best. The weeds were tall and tough. Angled and trapped against stones, they failed to come out whole. The thwarted life force seemed to knot and push the stems up thicker, even while she tugged at them. Kirsty prised out the stones embedded in the soil, like nuts in hard toffee, and found more lodged in the layer underneath. They scraped against the fork. She could see Luka's feet out of the corner of her eye but the rootedness that she had observed in him through the kitchen window seemed more tolerable at ground level. She sensed that he was happy to watch her and after a time she forgot that he was there. When she stood up to stretch her legs, she broke the silence to ask about the hospital. Luka described his duties but left out the smells and pathetic sights. 'Is it all right dealing with sick people, hour after hour?' she asked.

'It is best to be well,' he said. 'Like you and me.' Luka smiled as if the thought of their health gave him pleasure.

The calm ended when Abe appeared. Then Kirsty would have preferred large dogs around the place. The two men took up too much space and played a territorial game of pretending that the other had no right to be there. Abe talked non-stop and Luka was the silent statue – but it was the same game. Kirsty didn't know whether she was supposed to be referee, spectator or prize.

6

As she had warned, Paula did not return to London in time for Prayer Clinic on 3 June. She rang Vivienne at midday from a restaurant in Picardy. The weather was glorious. The restaurant had a Michelin star. She and Hartley hadn't even started on what they'd ordered, although the waiter had brought round *flamiche* – an upmarket kind of leek tart – as an appetiser. She said she could see lunch taking rather a long time and then Hartley would need a snooze in a field, before driving on to the Channel tunnel. That would take them until, say, six o'clock at the earliest and they still wouldn't have left France. Vivienne sighed when she put down the phone.

She arrived at Hilly's flat at about six thirty. A few of the group were already installed. Cushions had been set out in a circle on the floor and, although it was sunny outside, the blinds had been pulled down and tea lights had been set out in saucers and placed around the room. Hilly had no piano but Jennifer Patterson had brought her son's recorder along. Another woman, Dawn, who was fairly new to the group, was singing along to it, as she went round lighting the tea lights with a taper: ''Tis the gift to be simple,'tis the gift to be free. 'Tis the gift to come down where you ought to be. And when we find ourselves in the place just right, 'twill be in the valley of love and delight.'

Vivienne sat down on a tapestry cushion and waited for everyone to arrive and settle. Jennifer Patterson carried on playing and Dawn sang quietly. She had now joined the circle on the floor. 'When true simplicity is gained, to bow and to bend we shan't be ashamed. To turn, turn, will be our delight, till by turning, turning, we come out right.' Hilly had left the door of the flat ajar so that people could walk in without using the doorbell. Shoes were left by the door. The tradition was that there were no greetings, though nearly all the women smiled as they entered. Eventually, when most of the cushions were occupied, Hilly shut the front door and sat down herself. Jennifer brought 'Simple Gifts' to a close. There was silence.

This was the part of the evening that Vivienne liked best, after the music had ended and before anyone spoke. The room and the candles and the faces arranged themselves in an impersonal pattern. There was a freedom in the moment that promised nothing. She was reluctant to disturb it; to unleash goodwill into the silence. Wasn't there something coercive even about goodwill – the need to manipulate, to change? She let the minutes pass without any precise sense of time and, since no one fidgeted, for a little longer still. She heard the lift called to the next floor of the building and then descend. She opened the session with a short prayer and offered the meeting to Jesus.

They began with Becky, who had an eating disorder. She was the daughter of one of Hilly's friends. Then Dawn's parents, who had recently retired and were getting on each other's nerves. Ross, who had the rare cancer, and his wife Julia. They progressed through illness, divorce, financial difficulties. There was an underside to life even for prosperous people. Some of the information given was quite specific and first names were used. Vivienne felt unsure about some of the petitions relating to third parties – whether they weren't a betrayal of trust. She herself, at a previous meeting, had prayed for her next-door neighbour, Lynette, the one whose husband had left. Even as she had spoken she had regretted it. She had thought that she should have changed the name and some of the details but that had seemed wrong too – to give Jesus inaccurate data. Though, of course, He knew it all anyway. He knew everything.

Gaps eventually opened up between prayers. At this stage certain women spoke for the sake of speaking and it was better to call a halt before that happened. On the other hand there might be someone in the circle who had been summoning up the courage to give voice to a particular problem. Vivienne waited. In two days' time she would be in Sussex. She hadn't revisited the subject of Richard travelling down separately. His diary had accumulated even more dinners. He was out at one now. She thought of him, standing by the window during what she thought of as their quarrel after he had kept the girls waiting at the tennis club. She had tried to read his profile; the eye on the visible side of his face moving, scanning the sky – for what she didn't know. A rescue helicopter, perhaps. *Ask, and it shall be given you; seek, and ye shall find; knock, and it shall be opened unto you.* The advice seemed not to apply to her enquiries, or at least not to the finicky questions she had asked Richard. Vivienne was prepared to believe that other people managed things better. Paula, for instance, at that very moment returning from Normandy, would have known what to say to Hartley. She would have launched into the conversation in total confidence and in no time they would have been laughing together.

Vivienne cleared her throat. She had to recall all the people they had prayed for and name each one again. She decided that when she reached the end of the list, she would add Richard, out at his business dinner. It seemed to her that she hadn't been quite fair to him, resenting that he hadn't taken time off on Friday. She was lucky he was coming to Sussex at all. She felt renewed sympathy for Richard and suddenly – quite separate from the sympathy, sharply disconnected from it – a queasy feeling of love. The silence continued. Vivienne realised that she should speak, should probably have spoken some minutes earlier. She began the closing prayer, but something obstructed her train of thought. For the first time since she had been married, it occurred to her that Richard might not be where he said he was. As she said 'Heavenly Father', the words 'business dinner', which for her entire life she had regarded quite neutrally, stuck in her throat. Vivienne stopped in mid-sentence and swallowed hard. She saw Richard's hands resting on a white tablecloth and another woman looking at them. She raised her head and glanced around the circle. She saw Bellsie opposite her, her billowing skirt spread round her, concealing the cushion. Her eyes were wide open, reflecting the candlelight and she was looking at Vivienne with compassion.

Hilly had laid on wine and a selection of carrots, crisps and celery to dip into hummus and taramasalata. She began to bring the dishes through to the living room. The group had resolved to keep the post-prayer catering simple. It was so easy for canapé-making to become competitive. Vivienne usually stayed to socialise but she made her excuses and said goodbye. She found her shoes in the hall and slipped her feet into them. The women were talking and laughing. She went out and shut the door behind her without calling goodbye again. In the lift, she took out her phone and checked her messages. There was one from Paula saying she and Hartley were having dinner at a château in the Pas de Calais. Vivienne erased the message and tried calling Richard but his phone was switched off.

Henka was reading a novel and eating an apple when Vivienne returned. The girl looked isolated, sitting alone on one of the bench seats, with a straight back. All the ceiling lights were on.

'Henka, you should have made yourself comfortable in the sitting room. You don't have to stay in the kitchen,' Vivienne said.

'Here it is more cosy,' Henka said.

'Is that a good book?' Vivienne asked.

'Yes. Very good. It is Polish. I may go now?'

'Yes, of course you may, Henka. Did the girls get to bed all right?'

Henka was strict about bedtime. Eight o'clock sharp. The girls were tired after school. 'No problem,' Henka said. 'Their homework is complete. It is on the kitchen table.' She stood up and put on the thin jacket which had lain beside her, ready for wearing. 'I will say goodbye then.'

'Yes, thank you so much, Henka.' Vivienne delved into her bag and took out her wallet. She paid Henka by cheque at the end of the month – babysitting was extra. She put a note in Henka's hand and wished that there were a less obvious way of making the transaction. Henka looked at the note before placing it in her pocket. As if I might be cheating her, Vivienne thought sadly.

After Henka had left, Vivienne went into the study and switched on the radio – *Play of the Month* – but she wasn't listening. Odd phrases slipped through her inattention – '*You wore that dress when you were with my father in Capri, didn't you?*' – but she failed to pick up the thread of the story. She went over to the desk and opened it. The contents were inert, conveying nothing, not even giving back to her an awareness of her own intentions. She picked up Richard's wallet and took out the card printed with the feather. She turned it over, wrote down the telephone number on a scrap of paper and put the card back. It was best to do this thing quickly. Vivienne placed the wallet against her cheek. The deep red clematis was flowering, spilling out from its supporting wires; its blooms black against the edge of the window. Lynette's boys were on the trampoline in the next-door garden. Vivienne heard the thuds and every few seconds the top of a head appeared over the fence. As she breathed in the smell of old coins and leather, she wished she had stayed in the kitchen ... read a novel ... eaten an apple.

7

Abe stretched out on the swivel chair in his living room, with the portable electric fan whirring beside him. He tried to tune out the road and focus on the sounds that were coming through the landing window at the back of the house; neighbours' televisions, children screaming and, eventually, the rush of a watering can being filled from the tap. A blackbird began to whistle, as if in response to the sprinkling of water on leaves, then a police siren started up and that was the end of the birdsong. The plant waterer was Kirsty. No one else in the terrace went in for suburban behaviour. The first thing she did on returning home was to open the back door and step outside. Abe had got into the habit of wandering down to talk to her on the evenings he was at home. At the sound of the watering he got up from the chair and looked around for his cigarettes. He picked up his keys and went down the stairs. The fan carried on running.

Luka was leaning against a post of the broken fence smoking a roll-up, holding it cautiously, as if it might fall apart. The sun had almost gone from the garden. There was a corner that was still lit up and glowing pink, but Luka was in the shade. He had no shirt on and the waistband of his jeans hung low on his belly, showing the sharp tops of his hip bones. Against the drone of the traffic, Abe could hear the outside tap running. Kirsty emerged from the side of the house, staggering, with a plastic can slopping with water, which she aimed towards a clump of grey-green leaves. She was wearing a T-shirt threaded with ribbon and a tiny, fragile-looking skirt. She ignored Abe standing in the doorway. The drops formed miniature pools in the creases of the leaves, then dripped on to the dry soil beneath the plants. As the can became lighter, she waved it around more freely, cascading an arc of water over random pots and wetting Luka's feet. Luka shuffled. When the can was empty Kirsty went back into the alleyway. The tap was turned on again and this time Abe heard the force of the pent-up pressure as the water was released. He stepped forward and picked up a football that had landed on the paving and chucked it back over the fence, then he slid down on to the doorstep and put his face up to the sky. Unappetising smells of other people's dinners drifted out of nearby windows.

'Isn't the garden wet enough?' Abe asked when Kirsty reappeared with another brimming can of water.

'No, it isn't. What do you want?' she said.

'A cold beer would be good.' Abe stretched out his legs, making himself comfortable.

'Beer's all gone,' Kirsty said. She rained water down on her plants until the area of concrete between the house and the patchy grass was turning black and giving off a miasma like wet swimming kit. You could smell the chlorine in the London supply in hot weather.

'Luka needs to get down to the off licence. Keep you stocked up,' Abe said. He drew his left foot towards him and examined it, showing its grubby underside. He started to pick out pieces of stone and wet grass that had got stuck between his toes.

'Why not you?' Kirsty said. She pushed past Abe on the back step and went into the kitchen.

So far Luka hadn't looked in Abe's direction. Even talking about him failed to produce a response. Abe listened to the clatter of pans being put away, cupboard doors opening and shutting. Then, at last, a CD slotted into the machine, the volume turned up, the fridge door opened, the sound of a bottle placed on the table.

'Do you need a hand, Kirstabel?'

'No,' she said.

Abe got up all the same and stood in the doorway. 'I was only asking.'

Kirsty was unpacking the food she had bought from the supermarket and piling it up next to the wine bottle.

'How are my fish?' Abe went over to stick his finger in the water.

'Rallying,' she said.

Abe walked over to the cupboard and took out three glasses.

'What are you doing, Abe?'

'Getting some glasses out.' He held one in one hand and two in the other.

Kirsty turned round and made a face at him. It was exclusively his and had simplified over the years. There had once been some variations and experimentations. Now, like an artist at the height of her powers, she had pared the 'face' down to one or two telling lines.

'What's that for?' he said.

'Please, Abe, just go away.'

'Go away?'

Kirsty was taking a tray of chicken pieces out of the bag. She made various decent chicken dishes. Her telephone rang. She picked it up, tucked it to her ear with one hand and carried on unpacking with the other. After listening for a few seconds she said, 'No, sorry ... Sorry, I don't know who you're talking about. I think you've got the wrong number.' She put the phone down.

'Who was that?' Abe said.

'Someone called Vivienne.'

'Did she want Neil?'

'No. She said she wanted Richard Epworth.'

'Richard Epworth,' Abe repeated. The name seemed

familiar. He looked hopefully at the shopping as it emerged, anticipating the wish list of ingredients. So far, no lime or coriander. But there were other promising things. He remembered who Richard was. 'Ah,' he said, before he could stop himself.

Kirsty was on to him straight away. 'That means something to you, does it, Abe?' She stared at him. 'It does, doesn't it?'

'Don't worry. Forget about it.'

'So who is Richard Epworth?' Kirsty asked, separating the names for emphasis. She stopped, poised with a packet of pitta bread in her hand. 'Abe?'

He looked exaggeratedly blank.

Kirsty's memory clocked in. 'Is he the man you went home with in the taxi?'

'Any particular one you have in mind?'

'Abe. How did this woman, Vivienne, get hold of my number?'

Abe shrugged his shoulders.

'Who is she?' Kirsty persisted.

'A wife, perhaps.' Abe laughed. 'Or a sister.'

Suddenly Kirsty went into reverse. She stuffed the packet of pitta bread and the tray of chicken back into the bag, then the carton of milk, the cucumber and the tub of plain yoghurt. She crammed them all into the bag and tied it in a tight knot at the top.

'You'll need scissors for that now,' Abe said.

Kirsty went to the fridge, opened the door and forced the bag inside. 'Go away, Abe. Please. Just go.'

Abe stood looking at Kirsty, puzzled. Then, as her mood seemed fixed, he left the room and went upstairs.

In the upper part of the house the air had cooled a little. Abe leant out of the open window to smoke. He looked out at the rooftops opposite and listened to the passing traffic. Vivienne, he thought. He had forgotten that name. She had been skiing and must have been back for months. He remembered a photo of the daughters – the masks and Hallowe'en hats – but he had no picture of their mother. If any had been on display he couldn't recall one. Richard's wife had rung up Kirsty. How bizarre was that! He gave a single shout of laughter before taking another drag on his cigarette. Of course, since it was Kirsty's number he had given Richard, that wasn't totally remarkable, but the mini-conversation between the two women still struck him as incongruous. If he hadn't been with Kirsty when Vivienne called, he might never have known about it. He felt, for a moment, disconcerted at the thought of the odd conjunctions and coincidences that happened without his being there. Perhaps that was the essence of a coincidence, that someone in the know was there to take notice. A bus stopped in front of the house. Abe scanned the top deck. Nearly all the seats were occupied. Several people stared back at him. He half expected another example of synchronism but he didn't recognise any of the gawping faces. It was only when the road was clear again that it crossed his mind that something must have happened in the Epworth household to cause Richard's wife to ring the number. Without coming up with any specific scenarios, he wondered for the first time if there had been repercussions from his January trip.

8

As soon as Abe had left the room and was out of earshot, Kirsty picked up her phone. She found the number of the previous dialler and called back. The woman who replied was hesitant. She said she was Vivienne Epworth. She confirmed that she had rung a few minutes ago. Kirsty placed one bare foot on top of the other. 'I think you need my brother, Abe Rivers,' she said. 'He's not here now. I'll tell you where he'll be tomorrow, though.' She gave her Abe's mobile number and the name and address of Karumi, the sports injury treatment centre in Shoreditch.

After the call, Luka came in from the garden. He showed no curiosity about whom Kirsty had been speaking to, though her voice had been audible through the open door. She switched off the phone. Luka went across to the small canvas rucksack that he carried around with him. It was hanging over a chair. 'I've bought you a horse. Do you want to see it?' he said. So far he hadn't paid for anything, apart from six cans of ginger beer and a packet of economy bacon. Luka put his hand in the rucksack and took out a tiny black-and-white object tufted with yellow hair. He was turning a key on the toy's underside and placing it on the table. The mechanical horse stuttered a few centimetres and stopped. Its mane covered its face and its tail stuck out like a brush. 'It was working before,' Luka said.

'Let's go and sit upstairs. I'm fed up with being down here,' Kirsty said. She was still furious with Abe. The woman's polite tone and her own abrasive one echoed in her head.

'Don't we eat?' Luka said. 'No food?'

'No food. I'll bring the wine. You carry the glasses.' Kirsty moved to the table and picked up the bottle, which had now lost its chill. She took her time opening it, turning the corkscrew slowly.

Kirsty went upstairs to the living room, carrying the bottle. She stood it on the mantelpiece and glanced at herself in the mirror above that hung from a huge iron nail. She remembered how she and Marlene used to sunbathe, splayed out on the sports field, their skirts hitched up and their school ties, worn like Alice bands, holding their hair back from their glowing faces. By the end of the summer term her hair and skin were only a subtle shade apart. Now she looked pale and her eyebrows were witchily fierce. She filled the two glasses and handed one to Luka. He was sitting on the floor nursing the toy horse.

'Is it a palomino?' Kirsty said, making an effort.

'They have blond hair, yes. But their bodies are not black and white,' Luka said.

'What is black and white?'

'Friesian. Or is that cows? I will find out on the Internet.' Luka crouched down, turned the key in the horse. 'I got it in the market,' he said, looking up at her. Kirsty suspected the 'under a pound' shop. Luka had said market because he knew she liked markets. 'It will work,' he said. He put the horse on the rug, then on a bare piece of floor. It still didn't move.

Kirsty finished her glass of wine and poured herself another. 'Is it dead?' she asked. 'Or asleep? I know how it feels.' She knelt down beside Luka. The floorboards were warm from the afternoon sun. It was late now and growing dark but the boards retained the heat. Kirsty was tired and had drunk too fast on an empty stomach. She leant forward and rested her forehead on her folded arms, making a neat, prayerful shape. After a few minutes she drifted into a hazy state, half asleep, half awake.

An articulated lorry clattered to a stop outside the house. Kirsty surfaced and wondered how long she had been dozing. She felt relaxed but no longer dead. She was aware of Luka nearby, the flimsiness of her short skirt, her bare legs tucked underneath her and the good feeling of the skin of her thighs on the back of her calves. In her sleepy state the warmth of her flesh and the proximity of Luka merged into the same sensation – a kind of tactile humming. Keeping her eyes closed, she moved a fraction nearer. Why complicate life? and Why not? she thought. She repeated both questions in her mind until they made no sense. She shifted herself so that her legs were touching the edge of Luka's jeans. She could feel the stitching. He still wants me, she thought. She opened her eyes and looked sideways at Luka. He was turned away from her, she couldn't see his face. She raised herself on an elbow and touched his bare back with the tips of her fingers.

'Sodding horse!' he said, banging it down on to the floor.

Kirsty sat straight up, as if she had been burnt.

'What?' he asked.

'Nothing,' she answered.

'Why is it broken?'

'You must have overwound it,' she said dismissively, sitting on the hand that had reached for him.

'That's terrible,' Luka said. 'Not even crap goods. My own fault.' He held out the horse to Kirsty. 'You try.'

Kirsty snatched it from him. The key wouldn't budge going clockwise. She tried anticlockwise but there was no bite to it. The winding stem got looser and looser and dropped out.

'That's it,' she said. 'Kaput.'

They sat crossed-legged and looked at each other. Kirsty had nothing to say.

'What did Abe do?' Luka asked.

'What did Abe do when?'

'To make you so angry.'

Kirsty shrugged her shoulders. 'He gave my number to someone – instead of his own. I assume that's what happened anyway. He's done it before.'

'*Why* does he do this?'

'He doesn't like to be harassed.'

'So you are harassed. Great.'

'That's the general idea. Once he gave my number to the economics teacher at school who fancied him. Mr Owen.'

'You shouldn't allow him, Kirsty. It's wrong.'

'That's Abe. He's always been like that.' Kirsty did her best to sound nonchalant.

Luka stretched his hand along the floor towards her feet without making contact. 'Sorry for the horse,' he said.

'Don't worry about it. Why be sorry?'

'It was a present for you because I know that I'm a nuisance,' he said, slowly and correctly.

Kirsty took a deep breath. 'I like anything with hair. I'll take it anyway,' she said. She got up from the floor, tweaking the yellow mane between her fingers. She went over to the bookshelves and squashed the horse in between Neil's tatty collection of thrillers. Her own newer and still unfaded books were on the shelf below. Luka was watching her. The horse wasn't well displayed, so Kirsty spent a few minutes rearranging the paperbacks to give the creature more space. She heard a voice in her head, saying, 'You, Kirsty Rivers, would be good with children.' She struck a *tableau vivant* pose, spreading her arms wide, introducing the arrangement. She glanced at Luka. He was looking serious. What else was she supposed to do with the bloody horse? She remembered this about Luka, that when she was trying her hardest to keep him happy over some minor thing he seemed cosmically disappointed, as if the thing, whatever it was, had eternal significance that was beyond her grasp. She shrugged her shoulders.

'Do you still like *my* hair?' Luka asked.

'Yes, of course I do,' Kirsty said briskly.

Luka smiled.

Four

1

Unlike the new glass structures to the south of Liverpool Street Station, the Victorian warehouses to the north-west of the railway lines had fully opening windows. If you had to be stuck indoors on a June afternoon, Karumi wasn't a bad place to be. An old-fashioned electric fan hung from the high ceiling, revolving at the moderate speed of a long-playing vinyl record. Blinds made of Japanese paper were drawn against the sun.

There had been a bit of a rush on in the early part of the lunch period but by three thirty only two clients were waiting. One of them was restless, unaffected by the ambient calm. She got up from the leather sofa, sat down again, rearranged her scarf. Then she addressed Abe who was sitting behind the slate-topped table. 'Please call through and tell Mr Ibrahim I am here,' she said.

Abe took a swig from the large bottle of mineral water that was placed in front of him. 'Sorry, there's no intercom,' he said. 'Tariq will be out soon. He's running a few minutes late.' Abe felt under the table for the volume control on the sound system and the Buddhist monks lurched on to a new plateau of song. He stared at the computer and idled over his telephone messages. Impatience was probably what brought the woman here in the first place – fidgeting so much that she injured herself. Now she was applying dark lipstick, holding up a small gold compact mirror as if it were a fist. Abe yawned. He heard Tariq Ibrahim's voice, as the door opened: 'Take two ibuprofen, Mr Jenson. The discomfort will soon pass. No caving or pot-holing this weekend, no team-building exercises with that bank you work for. I make my living from company Away Days. Confine your speleology to videos.' A man in his late twenties, holding his jacket by its collar, preceded Tariq out of the treatment room. He was wearing a shirt with a wide stripe and his free arm was crossed over his chest, kneading the opposite shoulder with slow circular movements.

'Ah, Mrs Paz. Come along in,' Tariq said. He used only titles and surnames. It was a little bit of Harley Street come to EC2. Mrs Paz allowed herself to be shepherded through the door. Before shutting it, Tariq put his head back round and stuck his fingers in his ears. Abe turned the volume of the sound system down to a murmur. Mr Jenson punched in his pin number. He had a certain appeal, Abe thought. The earlier lunchtime clients had all been pimply megaphones in red ties; the type who ended the day in All Bar One. Mr Jenson had good skin and didn't crash around the place. Abe stared at his back and the crumpled shirt cloth as he disappeared through the exit. He heard the clanking of the lift rising to the top floor, the slam of the gate shutting, the clanking as it descended. Then it was quiet again.

A couple of minutes after Mr Jenson's departure the remaining client, a woman, put the magazine she had been leafing through to one side and stood up. She adjusted the sunglasses that rested on her head and walked towards Abe. 'Abe Rivers?' she said. Her voice sounded brittle and a little bit posh. Abe had never seen her before and was surprised to be addressed by name. She placed the fingertips of her left hand on the edge of the table, as if to steady herself. Her nails were painted impeccably. She wore a wedding ring and a circlet of sapphires and diamonds above it: what people call an eternity ring. 'I'm sorry to bother you. You don't know me and I haven't come for a ... treatment.' She hesitated over the word, came to a stop and started again. 'Vivienne Epworth,' she said.

Abe stared up at her. Mr Jenson was wiped from his mind. The woman in front of him had a childlike face – open but anxious – that seemed at odds with her well-groomed, almost glamorous appearance. She wasn't tall and carried herself straight to gain an extra half-inch. Abe smiled at her – the sort of smile that took up a little time. His face stretched into it and seemed to get stuck. 'Vivienne. Pleased to meet you.' He stood up, as if in a dream, and shook her hand across the table.

'Does my husband's name, Richard Epworth, mean anything to you?' she asked.

'Should it?' Abe said.

'Your sister said it would.'

'Kirsty? *Did* she? What did she say?'

Vivienne Epworth opened the clasp of her bag and seemed to be searching for something. Abe watched in silence. He blamed Kirsty for Vivienne's surprise visit but blame was no help to him. A deep channel was opening up in his mind. Its depth was unknown – and the direction of the flow. Vivienne had found what she wanted. 'I'd be very grateful if you'd just look at this.' A card fluttered in her hand. Abe took it from her. He glanced at it and handed it back. He had forgotten the feather; it was a nice design. It meant something, though he struggled to remember what. The woman herself was like a spiky kind of feather, or even more a bird that had become trapped indoors.

'Excuse me for saying this, but you seem a bit worried. Are you worried?' Abe said.

Vivienne gave a shake of her head that involved a kind of smile. It was as if she couldn't do one without the other.

'I don't want you to be worried. Let's go and sit down over there.' Abe indicated the sofa opposite. He came out from behind the table. Vivienne walked to the sofa and sat down. She took the sunglasses from her head and held them in her lap with the card. Abe tried to focus. The room seemed to have closed in on him, though the windows were open and the paper blinds that hung over them moved and tapped against the glass. 'Do you know anything about my sister?' he asked, turning towards Vivienne.

'No,' she said.

'I thought she'd already had a chat with you?' Abe paused but Vivienne offered no information. He wished he could make her look at him. She kept giving him quick alarmed glances that jigged him around as if he were shots taken by a hand-held camera.

'Kirsty can be a bit weird,' he said. 'Did she – kind of – say really odd stuff?'

'She seemed annoyed that I'd bothered her – which I fully understand.'

'She told you to come here. Did she explain why?'

'No. I've no idea why. I'm hoping you'll tell me.'

Abe took a breath and blew the air slowly from his mouth. He wanted to thank Kirsty as well as kill her. Vivienne shifted slightly next to him. Abe looked at the small ringed hand gripping the card. Now he had to get her out without harming her. He didn't have much material to work with. Kirsty, feather. Kirsty, bird. He flipped to peace and pet shops in a wild game of associations. Steady on, he told himself.

'Kirsty has talent. Same as our dad. He was an artist, a photographer. He took a photo of a girl leaning over Waterloo Bridge. Perhaps you know it?'

'No,' Vivienne said.

'Before your time, probably. The girl's name was Tamsin Spira. The poster made her quite famous for a while. When you look at the photo you're not sure whether she's on her way home after a night out – just stopping on the bridge to look at the dawn – or about to jump. Kirsty's quiet – not like me – but one day she'll do something good like that. Music, though, not photography. It's typical of her to have chosen a feather. Something that's small and insignificant and floats through the air or on water ... ' Abe took a breath. '... And that weighs nothing at all.' A memory returned, like a thread of light underneath a door. He had to keep going and sensed that there would be something round a corner to save him. The feather had a meaning connected with Gloria. 'Osiris,' Abe said and dried up.

Vivienne gave him another of her choppy looks.

'You've heard of Osiris?' Abe continued, in what he hoped was a normal voice. More of the stuff was coming back to him. Gloria's chanting – the Egyptian judgement of the dead.

'Well, I know he was an Egyptian god.' Vivienne's face turned pink. 'But is it another word for something?'

'Not as far as I know. What sort of thing?'

Vivienne shook her head. She hesitated. 'Is it something people take?'

Abe stared at her. He felt that he had been put in charge of a vessel made of glass and, although Vivienne looked the young side of middle-aged, it seemed like very old glass, all the more fragile for having survived so long undamaged. 'If it is, they haven't told me about it. Osiris was a saviour god who died and rose to life,' he said. He never had made Gloria the website.

'I don't think so,' Vivienne said quickly. 'Only one person did that.'

Abe remembered the Epworth noticeboard. He nodded slowly. 'I think I see where you're coming from. But we can share, can't we? Pool our resources?'

Vivienne crossed her legs. She was wearing heeled sandals and her toenails were the same pink as the paint on her fingers. Abe waited a moment while his memory fully clocked in – but not too long. She was becoming impatient. 'The feather is truth,' he said. 'After death a person has to give an account of his or her life and what counts isn't what he or she has, or has not, done but how truthful the account is. They called it negative confession. The person's heart is weighed against truth. That's a *really* interesting idea, isn't it?'

'Up to a point,' Vivienne conceded, 'but I can't see what it's got to do with your sister – or Richard.'

Voices behind the left-hand door indicated that the session had come to an end. Abe didn't want Tariq getting involved in this. 'I need water,' he said. 'Do you want some? Or I could make you a peppermint tea?' Vivienne shook her head. Abe stood up and went to the table. He picked up the bottle and took a gulp. The coldness trickled down his throat without refreshing him. He wiped his mouth with the back of his hand.

The door opened. It stayed ajar for a few moments, then Mrs Paz and Tariq came out. 'No more weights, Mrs Paz,' Tariq was saying. 'No more suspending Mr Paz from the balcony. Abe will make you another appointment for the same time next week. We'll take it from there, Mrs Paz. See how it goes. Little and often will be our motto.' Mrs Paz looked mournful. Her scarf hung slackly round her neck. She limped towards the exit. 'Take the stairs, Mrs Paz. Stairs are sovereign,' Tariq called after her. They heard the clanking of the lift rising to the top floor, then the slam of the gate shutting, then the clanking again as it descended.

'Mrs ... ?' Tariq said, cocking his head to one side and looking down at Vivienne.

'Epworth. I'm not a client.'

'Vivienne just dropped by,' Abe said. 'We're having a chat.'

'Good, good. I can stop work then, can I?' Tariq went back into his room without waiting for an answer and returned a few minutes later without the white coat. 'I'll just go and grab a coffee, Abe. I'll be back in ten minutes.'

'Ta-ta, then.'

'Ta-ta, as you say, Abe.'

Throughout the interruption Vivienne had been turning her rings round and round on her finger.

'The thing is ... ' Abe said, sitting down again, but closer to Vivienne this time. 'Poor Kirsty's having a bit of a crisis. She started the Osiris group but then she couldn't deal with it.' He looked at the space between his feet. 'She went too far with the whole spiritual bit. She was fasting and chanting – which is cool – but she overdid it. Started hyperventilating, having nightmares that she was locked in a tomb. All that kind of thing. I don't know if you've ever had a bad trip?' He lifted his head.

'No,' Vivienne said. 'I haven't.' She was staring at him, astonished.

'I've been really worried about her. I haven't either, by the way. And I was gutted about all the effort she'd put into the group. She was doing really well up to that point. I didn't want the whole thing to fold when she'd only just got started so I said I'd take over – talk to anyone who showed an interest and keep them posted. Until she was better. That's it, really. I mean, I'm not totally convinced by every aspect. "*His sun disc is your sun disc, His rays are your rays*," Abe intoned at this point. 'All that I find a bit turgid. But I'm committed. Definitely committed. I do it for her because she's my sister.'

Vivienne didn't reply immediately. 'It never occurred to me that she was ill,' she said. 'Or involved in a cult.'

'To be honest, Vivienne, you're not the ideal punter. You've got your own belief system. A lot of the people who get in touch just want to talk about their problems. I feel like saying, "I don't want to hear about your crappy existence. Sort yourself out." That's not right, is it, when they're searching for the truth?'

'You seem to be doing your best,' Vivienne said.

'Frankly, I've got enough to do keeping my own life together, without taking on anyone else's.'

Vivienne nodded. 'Do you think your sister might have given my husband the card?' she asked tentatively.

'Sorry? Oh yes. Hundred per cent. I was forgetting it

wasn't you Kirsty had given the card to. She was always handing them out. Tube stations, banks, bars. You name it, she was there.'

'But there's no information on them.'

'She likes to keep it personal. After her chat, as long as the person isn't a nutter, she puts her number on the back. She has to be careful because of running the groups from home. There are a lot of weirdos about. She obviously thought your husband was the trustworthy sort.'

'He is,' Vivienne said. 'Totally.' Her expression was still puzzled but the diffused redness had shrunk to two small blotches on her cheeks. She looked around the room, making an effort at curiosity. 'What *really* goes on here?' she asked.

'The usual stuff. Physiotherapy, acupuncture, osteopathy. What did you think went on?'

'I thought all kinds of stupid things. The entrance is misleading.' She paused. 'But it's pleasant once you get up here.' She looked towards the stone bowl and glugging water with a professional eye.

'I'm glad you like it,' Abe said. 'I'd recommend Tariq. He's the osteopath. Different practitioners come and go throughout the week. They rent the rooms. But Tariq's the best. If you ever have a bad back or anything, you should see him. Definitely. Do you work near here?'

'Ruislip. If you know where that is.'

'Out west somewhere, isn't it? Probably a bit too far to come with a slipped disc.'

Vivienne smiled.

'I knew you weren't the Shoreditch type. And you're too nice to work in the City,' Abe said. She *was* nice, since she had stopped being starchy. He got up and walked to the table. He picked up the bottle again. 'Sure you don't want some?' Vivienne shook her head. Abe raised the bottle to his lips, put it down again and returned to the sofa. He remained standing. 'It's been really good to meet you,' he said.

'You too.' Vivienne stood up and placed her sunglasses just above her forehead. She put out her hand but Abe ignored it. He gave her a hug. He looked down at the top of her head; the shiny hair that stayed put behind her ears – a different substance from Rivers hair. 'I feel I know you,' he said. He meant it. 'I'd appreciate some feedback. On the Osiris spiel. What did you think? You can be honest. Really. Please tell me. I like to learn.'

Vivienne skewed her lips to one side in concentration, trying to find the right words. 'You made me feel rather trapped. But that's probably just me.'

'Trapped isn't good. I'll have to do better,' he said.

'I don't believe in any of that esoteric rubbish – but you're streets ahead of me. I'm useless.'

'At what?' he asked.

Vivienne's shoulders hunched under the summer jacket. The action was more defeatist than a shrug. She saw Abe looking and straightened herself up.

'You came here,' Abe said. 'That was brave.' He walked with her across the room. He hoped her step was buoyant – though probably a brisk rise and fall was the only way to walk in those sandals. He wanted to think that she looked a different person from the one who had first approached him. He opened the door and Vivienne went out.

Abe returned to the table. He rested his elbows on the slate top and, cupping his hands, placed his two index fingers on the bridge of his nose. He could feel the heat of his breath. The conversation had gone all right, but for some reason he wasn't as relieved as he would have expected to be. He felt, without knowing exactly how, that he had let Richard down, as if he, not Richard, had been the older one and should have acted more responsibly. The thought disconcerted him. Whether he had slipped up in January, or just now, or at some time in between he wasn't quite sure. He remembered the stranger in the taxi offering him shelter and hospitality for the night; an offer made not exactly innocently, but in good faith. Abe passed his tongue over his lower lip. For a few minutes he concentrated, remaining quite still, apart from an errant muscle in the knee that had developed a life of its own. Then he removed his hands from his face and placed his fingers on the computer keyboard. He typed in the name of a well-known firm of City accountants and when the details came up on the screen he picked up the phone.

As he waited to be put through to Richard's secretary, Abe leant back and swung round slowly.

'Clare Sharpe,' a voice said. When Abe asked for Richard she said that he was in a client meeting and wondered if she could help. Abe said that it was a personal call. She said that if he left his number Richard would get back to him.

'Don't bother him, Clare,' Abe said. 'I'm going out any minute.' He hesitated, then he said, 'How is he?' She said he was well. She sounded surprised to be asked.

2

At six o'clock, Kirsty pulled down the roller shutter on the main part of the shop, leaving the front accessible to clients with keys to the mail boxes. For once, and perhaps because of the fine weather, she had no trouble dislodging the lingerers. The place had emptied itself. Kirsty walked along the roads behind Oxford Street towards the bus stop. She passed the waiters who sat in the shade on the back steps of the hotel. 'Hello. You-me have sex?' one called out.

'No chance,' Kirsty said. Although it was the end of the working day, the air was warm. The parks would be full of people lazing in deckchairs or lying in the sun, as the shadows tapered. It would be good to sit by water, Kirsty thought, or go swimming, or have a picnic. She took out her phone and left messages with Marlene and a couple of other friends. No one replied. She thought of Luka already leaning against the fence waiting for her – or perhaps just waiting. She wondered whether Gloria was in. She thought of the train to Crystal Palace in the rush hour; the crowds and the heat.

Gloria was sewing in the small garden at the back of the house when Kirsty arrived. The sewing machine was on the wooden table with its electric cable plugged in to an extension lead that snaked its way indoors to one of the kitchen plugs. Silky cloth, the oily colour of a dark pond, lay smoothly under the presser foot of the machine and rose and dipped into folds that hung over the table and almost touched the ground.

'I'll just finish this seam, Kirsty, then we'll have a drink,' Gloria said.

'Don't worry about me. You keep going. I'll sit on the grass,' Kirsty said.

'I haven't cut it yet this year,' Gloria said.

'I can see that.' Kirsty lay down on her back and was immediately hidden. The grass was thicker than in Iverdale Road and the weeds were frondy; not the low-growing tough rosettes that she struggled with at home. She pretended she was in a meadow. Although the garden was hemmed in by neighbouring houses, from her supine position Kirsty could see only the sky. An aeroplane crossed her field of vision, its engine noise masked by the whirring that started and stopped as Gloria depressed her foot on the pedal and raised it. Kirsty was lulled by the sound, though as a child she'd been maddened by it – another barrier to getting Gloria's attention. No one else's mother had made clothes for fun. That had been the eccentricity, not the heaving of the sewing machine out of doors. For all Kirsty had known, that was where all summertime sewing took place. Gloria used to make anything loose that could be stitched until, at about the age of seven, Kirsty had objected to the baggy floral trousers and gypsy skirts. She had wanted things with a bit of Lycra that you chose from rails in high street shops. The colours weren't as good. She admitted that now. Acidic or plain boring – high street colours. But never again – unless she borrowed Gloria's clothes – did she have to dress in shades it was hard to find a name for.

The whirring noise stopped. Through the grass, Kirsty could see that Gloria's foot was no longer on the pedal. She sat up. Gloria was snipping at a thread with the scissors. She stood up, folded the cloth into a pile and picked it up. 'Stay there, Kirsty. I'll go and get the wine,' she said.

Kirsty could see more of the garden now. The jasmine that

was draped over the fences, and which produced thousands of starry scented flowers later in the summer, was sprouting fresh dark leaves and stems tinged with red. Its branches hung down and met the grass, nearly concealing the sleeping Buddha who rested serenely on his stone bed, his eyes closed in perfect curves. Long ago, Kirsty used to wrap him in blankets. He kept his dignity, whatever she did to him. Gloria reappeared carrying the old tin tray with an open bottle of wine and two glasses, carefully balanced. She bent and put the tray on the grass next to Kirsty, flattening the stems. She sat down herself, her feet tucked under her and her skirt spreading out. Kirsty leant across and poured the wine. Gloria took a deep breath and smiled. 'This is nice.' She looked happy, Kirsty thought, less fierce than when they had lived at home with her. Gloria had been tenacious – working, bringing them up, but also hanging on to her music, her New Age hobbies, her occasional boyfriends. They were probably in that order of importance. Sometimes the hanging on had made her grim. It was clearly a relief to her that she no longer had to provide for her children. She didn't seem old, although she was their mother.

'How's the house?' Gloria asked.

'All right. I like it.'

'Weird to think of you there.'

'Do you mind?'

Gloria sipped the wine and looked thoughtful. 'No. It's just weird. Everything comes back in some way or other if you wait long enough.'

'Not everything?'

'Unexpected things,' Gloria said. 'The things you had thought had snapped right off. Anyway, it's a house. It was a waste, really, with just Neil in it.'

'There were tenants once, weren't there?'

'For a while there were people upstairs, an Irish couple, I can't remember their names, and then, when they left, a woman called Gaynor, who had callers – and a Siamese cat that used to streak up and down the stairs with its ears pinned back. It was nervous of Neil.'

'He probably kicked it.'

'No. He wouldn't have done that,' Gloria said.

'Abe and I thought of getting a cat but then he was given the fish.'

'How are they?'

'That's what Abe says. "How are my fish?"'

'After Gaynor, the upstairs was empty. Neil didn't bother,' Gloria said.

Kirsty liked to think of the tenants who came and went. And Gaynor's callers. From a distance, the arrangements seemed fluid. It was only when you had your nose pressed right in a situation that you thought it would last for ever. 'I'd like to have met the upstairs people. It would have made it more interesting. I could have played with the cat. Did it go in the garden?'

'Not as far as I know. It just went mad on the stairs.'

'The back door was always locked,' Kirsty said. 'The bolts were rusty.'

'You were always interested in the way doors were fastened.'

'Funny,' Kirsty said. She thought of her childhood self without sentiment; remembering herself not as photograph-sweet, but as empty – the inside of a person who is new enough to know nothing. She was still unsure how she was doing – filling the space.

'No one used the garden,' Gloria said. 'The only time I remember going out there was when Neil had a bonfire. He burnt a lot of old furniture. I can see him now, knocking the flaming pile into shape with a table leg so that it wouldn't fall into the fence and set it alight.'

'You make it sound like the Middle Ages.'

'It was a bit like that. Without the witches.'

Kirsty picked up a piece of the jasmine that was within reach. She held it between her two hands and tugged at its elastic strength. She realised she was crushing the new shoots and let the stem fall across her lap. 'We never liked going to see him,' she said. 'We didn't *hate* it, but there was nothing to do. He never made us a bonfire.'

'No. I thought he might get more interested in you as you got older. But it never happened. There was that time when you went there and he wasn't in. I was going to give him a bollocking about that but then I thought, why bother?'

'He didn't change?'

'No, he didn't change.'

This suddenly struck Kirsty as unlikely, given the bonfire. There must have been other flarings. The famous photograph of Tamsin had been one. There *must* have been others over a lifetime. Somehow, it had been convenient for all of them to think of Neil as a lost cause.

'Would it have made a difference if we'd tried harder?' she asked.

'You were children,' Gloria said.

'Children can try.'

'Yes and no.'

'He must have thought about us though – or he wouldn't have left us the house.'

'Yes. I don't know what went on in his head. I think he didn't want you to reject him. He preferred that you didn't know him at all. In the end, he gave you what he had. It could have been worse,' Gloria said.

'You've never said that before. About rejection.'

'I don't know what went on in his head.'

Kirsty stopped drinking after the second glass of wine. It would be a mistake to fall asleep on the train. She was glad that Gloria hadn't asked about Abe – and she herself hadn't mentioned Luka. Sometimes it was good not to talk about the present. She thought of Neil's own childhood. His father, the GI, who hadn't stayed in Britain once the Second World War ended. They had never had news of him. Neil's mother, Shirley, back in the late 1940s had wanted to forget everything about her American boyfriend. Women did that in those days – wished something had never happened, then lived the rest of their lives as if the wish had come true. She hadn't put her baby up for adoption, though. Shirley had focused on the hair and said her own sister's had been bushy – bushy was a forties word. And since her sister had gone to live in Belfast there was nothing to disprove it. She might well have had a perm that had gone wrong. Reality gives its support to odd causes.

The song that Kirsty had almost forgotten seemed as if it might get written – not in a rush of adrenalin but gradually, slowly, over the summer. If she became famous, or even if she didn't, she would dedicate it to Neil: 'In homage to Neil Rivers'. She felt fond of her house again. She wanted to get back there. She thought of the old furniture and was pleased that it hadn't all gone up in smoke. The lumpy sofa covered in Indian cloth – it seemed right that someone in need of a bed should be sleeping on it.

She and Gloria went inside and made some food – eggs on toast – and took it out into the garden to eat. Then, when they had finished, they carried the sewing machine into the kitchen because although it was still light, the shadows were long, stretched across from fence to fence, and the light wasn't good enough to sew by. Kirsty left soon afterwards and walked to the station.

3

It was about ten o'clock when Kirsty arrived back home. As she walked in, she could hear Abe's television on upstairs. The lower part of the house was quiet. Kirsty opened the door to the living room. The pillow and folded sleeping bag were in a neat pile on the floor but the zip-up bag had gone. She turned on the light and looked round the room. The yellow-haired horse was on the bookshelf where she had placed it the previous evening, crammed between the cracked spines of Neil's paperbacks. Otherwise everything was as it had always been: the sofa and chairs draped in Indian cloth, the threadbare rugs with their trailing fringes, the lifeless curtains. Two used wineglasses and an empty bottle stood on the floor. Kirsty went down to the kitchen. The back door was locked. There was no note. Notes are left in obvious places. She felt aggrieved that her hospitality was no longer required. She picked up her phone, about to call Luka, then stopped herself. She had wished him gone and now he was. It had been a safe kind of wish since she hadn't imagined it coming true – she had failed to put her back into it. She hadn't gone on to consider how she would feel if Luka left. Kirsty unbolted the back door and stepped outside, not knowing what to make of the changed situation. The garden smelled dry in spite of her manic watering the previous evening. She walked round to the tap and turned it on. The water gushed into the can and she regulated it to a more moderate pace. She filled the can seven or eight times and drenched her plants until they smelled green.

Kirsty went back into the kitchen. She was surprised to see Abe sitting at the table. She hadn't heard him come in, while she had been out in the garden.

'I hope you're pleased with yourself,' he said.

Kirsty had been about to say 'hi'.

'It feels good wrecking other people's lives, does it?' His voice was quite neutral, given what he was saying.

'I haven't wrecked anyone's life. What are you on about?'

'Think about it.'

'I'm going to make a cup of tea. Do you want one?' she asked. 'I went to see Mum after work.' Kirsty switched the kettle on. She took two mugs off the shelf and a new packet of tea bags from the cupboard. She started to remove the plastic covering, running a fingernail under the join.

'Righteous cow,' Abe said.

Kirsty's mood was calm. That didn't change. She was untouched by what Abe said. 'I'm making this tea for you,' she said when she heard the switch on the kettle click. 'If you don't want to stay for it, that's fine by me.'

'Some sort of control freak,' Abe said.

'Abe. Would you stop insulting me, or leave now. Please.'

'Do you really not remember?'

'Remember what?'

'Think about it.'

Kirsty poured the boiling water into one of the mugs. She held the kettle poised above the other one. 'Do you want this or not?'

'What is this, "control through tea"?' he said. 'You're not a fucking Japanese tea master. You've got your priorities wrong.'

'If you say so. But I don't go round insulting people for no reason.' Kirsty went to the fridge and took out the carton of milk. She poured a slug into the mug; some of it dribbled down the side.

'So it's all right to interfere in someone's marriage, is it? To tell a woman you've never even met that her husband is gay?'

Kirsty went still. 'I didn't do that.' She stared at Abe.

'As good as.'

'What happened?' she asked.

'Oh, so you want to know now, do you? You've remembered.' Abe stood up. He walked towards the door and before Kirsty had a chance to stop him he had left the room. She could hear him going up the short flight of steps to the hall. Let this not be real, she thought.

She heard Abe's feet on the next flight of stairs. She ran out of the room and up into the hall. 'Abe,' she called.

'What?' He stopped and turned round.

'I didn't mean it. I didn't mean it like that. Please tell me what happened.'

Abe stood on the top step, looking down.

'Please. Can't you be nice to me?' she begged.

'Nice to you? Why?'

'You've done stupid things too.'

Abe made some dismissive noise. He turned back again, went through his door and closed it behind him.

Kirsty went down to the basement and into her bedroom. She lay down on her bed. She felt as if her head were underwater and she would have to stay there until she drowned. At first she couldn't cry, then she started and couldn't stop. The noise and the heaving passed through her in waves. She didn't know where they kept coming from. She cried for the unknown couple and their children, if they had any. For Neil and Gloria and Luka and Abe. For herself. She was a thing that convulsed, a switchback, a wailing machine. She carried on and wore herself out. She fell asleep.

*

Kirsty woke up, sensing someone standing over her.

'Kirsty?'

She sat straight up. The lights were on and Luka was standing at the end of the bed. She was as shocked as if he had been a burglar.

'I thought you'd left,' she said, staring at him.

'I went to my cousin's in Luton but the children were ill. I couldn't stay. Why have you got your clothes on, Kirsty?'

'Luton. That's miles away. Why did you go there?' she asked.

'I thought you wanted me to go.'

'That's terrible,' Kirsty said. She looked down at herself – the crumpled skirt and T-shirt. Her feet were unwashed; grey as newspaper print on top of the white sheet.

'You've been crying. You weren't crying because of me, were you? ... Kirsty?' Luka moved to the side of the bed. As he came closer, she smelled the out-of-doors on him – London, night air and public transport. She smelled it on his shirt and on his hands. Kirsty remembered why she was still dressed and why she'd been crying. She wished she had been crying only for Luka. How simple that would have been. 'I'd better get up,' she said, pushing him.

'Why?' he asked.

'I can't stay here.' She stopped pushing but she felt the room closing in and Luka as the sentry to the exit.

'What do you mean? Kirsty, you're not making sense.'

'I don't know how to put it right. I can't put it right.' She tugged at a strand of wiry hair as if to measure the space she was confined in. Luka put his hand on her head. 'Don't touch me.' He took the hand away. 'No. Hold me,' she said.

Luka sat down on the edge of the bed and put his arms round her. She rested her head on his shoulder and closed her eyes. It was different with her eyes shut and Luka holding her. She was grateful. They stayed like that for several minutes. Luka's hand moved. He started to rub her back.

'Look, Kirsty,' he said in her ear, still rubbing, 'I shall turn the lights out. I'll come straight back. If you want to talk you can talk. Is that all right?' Kirsty nodded and Luka disengaged himself. She lay down and waited, still with her eyes closed. She could hear Luka go to the bedroom door. He switched off the light and the colour behind her eyelids changed. He went into the passage, then into the kitchen, turning off lights as he went. Finally it was dark. She heard him return. He shut the door behind him. There was some shuffling – he was taking his shoes off. He came over to the bed and lay down next to her. She shifted so that he could fit his arm underneath her. She moved close to him.

'Will you tell me?' Luka asked.

The seconds passed. Luka moved his shoulder to get comfortable. He adjusted the hand that rested on her, so that its position and pressure remained as before.

'You remember last night?' She spoke as if from the distant end of a tunnel.

'Yes.'

'The phone call I told you about?'

'Yes. I think so.' His ear brushed hers as he nodded.

Kirsty opened her eyes. She couldn't make herself understood with them shut. 'You must remember,' she said.

'Some gay guy, wasn't it? Friend of Abe,' Luka said.

'No. It was a woman. I rang her back and told her to go and see Abe. I was annoyed with Abe. That's why I did it.'

'Quite right. Abe gave her your number.'

'No, he didn't. He gave it to her husband,' she said quickly.

'Who cares? Abe shouldn't give your number to other people.'

'But it's a sort of joke. I *know* about it.'

Luka raised himself on the elbow that was underneath her and leant over her. 'What *happened*, Kirsty? I can't help you if you don't tell me.'

'I shouldn't have done it. It was none of my business.'

'But what happened?' His voice was too loud.

'Lie down,' she said. 'I don't like you up there. I can't think.'

Luka lay down flat. This time he held her hand. She thought of Abe three floors above and wondered if he was asleep. She told Luka what Abe had said. She remembered the conversation verbatim. She didn't exaggerate. When she had finished Luka took a deep breath. He moved his head from side to side as if he had a stiff neck.

'Kirsty,' he said. 'Nothing happened. Probably.'

'What do you mean?'

'You don't *know*. Abe didn't tell you. The woman, the wife, she goes to the clinic place. Maybe she has treatment.'

'No one has treatment if they don't need it. I keep telling you, she went to see *Abe*. I sent her. Why would Abe have said that stuff – that I'd wrecked people's lives – if it wasn't true?'

'Kirsty.' Luka made her name sound like a warning. He squeezed her hand tighter.

'Let go, that hurts,' she said. He relaxed his grip and she continued, 'I can bear anything – as long as it happens to me, not to other people.'

'Nice idea – but I don't think so.'

'Hearing the detail wouldn't change anything,' she said.

'Yes, of course it would. Some facts. He's just winding you up. Did you give the woman Abe's number?'

'Yes, I think so.'

'Then no worries. She called Abe and he told her to piss off.'

Kirsty shifted away from Luka. 'You just don't like him,' she said. 'I wish I hadn't told you.' Luka's reasonableness felt like an insult.

'Kirsty. Just think. Please. Even if this woman went to see Abe today – imagining whatever. Abe's as clever as fuck. He fixed it. If he can't do that, no one can.'

'No one can,' she repeated. 'Exactly.'

'Please don't start crying again. People like Abe can do anything,' Luka said, as the heaving began somewhere underneath Kirsty's ribcage. He put his arm underneath her again and pulled her closer. She fitted herself against him so that they touched each other all the way down to their feet. The heaving subsided.

Kirsty had a memory of standing in a crowd waiting for the fireworks to begin. It dated from childhood and came back to her, like a dream, when she was anxious. She saw sudden shafts of London and glittery sky. It was as if the wind were parting the branches of trees, revealing snatches of view. Abe, aged about eight, had disappeared – to find something he needed, he said. When he wormed his way back he was waving a lighted sparkler, clearing himself a space among the legs by writing his name. He stood in front of Kirsty in his dark parka with its furry hood – solid compared with the gusting faraway lights. He took a second wire out of his pocket and set it ablaze by touching the dull tip to the sparkling one. Kirsty forgot the fireworks, wanting only that the twinkly confusion of the sparklers would last for ever. Abe poked one of them at her and said, 'Take it, take it, are you scared or something?' Kirsty pressed her hands to her sides but in the end her right hand shot out and took hold of it. She had to concentrate to keep it tight without flinching as the sparks came nearer to her fingers. They were all she could see. She blocked out the world.

'Did you see that?' Abe shouted.

Kirsty held on.

'Didn't you see it?'

The burning end was almost at her fingertips. She stared at the spluttering light and willed it to stop. It edged closer. She felt a sharp, ice-cold pain and her hand flew open. She struggled to work out what anything meant. Because Abe was four years older, she pretended that she knew everything he knew. She still did. It was more painful than everyday lying; it felt more like holding her head underwater and realising she might have to stay there until she drowned.

'You saw it, didn't you? The big face made of fireworks,' Abe said.

Kirsty was still looking at the ground at the dead bit of wire.

'The mouth was big and orange and the eyes were green with black holes, like pupils, and it had big hair, like ours, and there were seven colours in it. All the colours,' Abe said.

Kirsty looked up at the sky and saw fountains and starbursts and sunbursts – wave after wave of them – and heard bangs that cracked open the night but she didn't see a face. She cried. She carried on crying all through the display and all the way to the bus stop.

'This is stupid, Kirst,' Gloria said. 'No one wants to hear you wailing. Just stop it before the bus comes, would you.'

She was sharing a cigarette with a boyfriend, Danny, who had come along for the occasion but she wasn't distracted. She was never distracted.

'Why are you smoking, Mum?' Abe asked.

'Because it's Bonfire Night,' Gloria answered.

'Kirsty didn't like the bangs,' Abe said in a sincere voice – sincerely concerned for his sister.

'They weren't especially loud,' Gloria said. 'It was pretty tame, really. They were louder last year. And there were hot dogs.'

'I did,' Kirsty said, between sobs. 'I liked them.'

'What's the matter with her?' Gloria asked.

'I missed it,' she wailed. 'That's all. That's all.'

'What did she miss?' Gloria ground the cigarette under her foot because the bus was coming.

'That's not your cigarette, Mum. It's Danny's,' Abe said.

'Mind your own business, Abe,' Gloria told him. 'If I want your advice I'll ask for it.'

'Kirsty wanted to see a face made of fireworks,' Abe said in a confiding voice but loud enough for the boyfriend to hear.

'He said there was. He said there was,' Kirsty screamed but no one understood her because her voice was distorted by grief.

'Why can't she enjoy what's in front of her?' Gloria said. 'It's Bonfire Night, for God's sake. Lighten up. All she has to do, for once, is enjoy what's in front of her.'

4

Martha had discovered among her grandmother's cast-off books a childhood relic – a book that began with blossom and ended with jam, though the middle section about black-berrying was, in her opinion, the best. Martha liked a clear narrative line without surprises and *The Tale of a Little Black Fruit* ticked the boxes. The book had been in good condition when Martha found it, having hardly been read in the last sixty-five years, but after a month of her ownership the spine was fractured and the ivory-coloured pages fell open automatically at 'Girls beware! The sweet black chap stains hands and hair.' Although Martha was past the age of shouting out in the supermarket, Vivienne had explained to her that other people, less enthralled by the work of Mildred Mary Dibbs, wouldn't necessarily enjoy hearing this said aloud.

The book had accompanied Martha to the rented cottage in Sussex and was lying on a lace-edged mat that covered the bedside table between the girls' single beds. They had discussed blackberries in the car on the way down. How charming, Vivienne had thought, that my children are talking about the hedgerows of Sussex. Some went round the farmers' fields and some went down to the edge of the sea. Birds lived in them, and hedgehogs and mice. They were made of different bushes all mixed up – holly and oak and honeysuckle and blackberry. At this time of year the blackberries were tiny and green – so tiny that you could hardly see them. Of course, everybody knew that at this time of year they were green. The conversation had rattled along. 'But that doesn't mean you can't pick them. You can't pick them to eat but you can pick them for the sake of picking,' Martha had said.

'You scum,' Bethany had said. 'Everybody knows you can't go blackberrying in June.' Frances had said that 'scum' was very, very rude. Martha and Bethany had started to fight. They had both screamed. Frances had done her best from the front seat, half turning round, with her seat belt straining – patting the writhing legs, interposing her veined hand between them, as they sped along the motorway in the fast lane. Frances had said that green blackberries helped to set jelly. She had said that there was a Scottish dinner called Amulree Grouse and that they very likely used green blackberries in that. She had said that Amulree Grouse had whisky in it too and that it was always a good idea to have a miniature bottle with you for moments like these. Vivienne had considered driving into the crash barrier to put an end to it all. She had yelled that she would have to stop driving if the noise carried on.

Now Martha was never going to leave the bedroom.

'We may as well eat with the girls,' Vivienne said. 'The sausages are nice. We'll have them with new potatoes and cauliflower. It will save cooking twice. We'll have a glass of wine when we eat.'

'I was rather banking on having one in the next five minutes,' Frances said. 'That bottle I popped in the freezer will be cold by now.'

'It's only half past five, Mummy,' Vivienne said.

'Well, it's my birthday tomorrow. And we deserve it. My goodness me, we deserve it, darling,' Frances said. 'We're both absolute saints, I think. Not to have throttled them.'

The cottage was solidly built on the outside but the inner partitions were flimsy. Vivienne had already ascertained that everything that happened downstairs could be heard above.

The grandfather clock, with flowers on its face, for example, seemed to tick in all the bedrooms, although it stood in the kitchen. Martha would be able to hear everything they said through the floorboards. 'Them,' Frances had said, 'throttled *them*.' That wouldn't go down well. Martha would only want Bethany throttled. Vivienne pointed upwards and made a warning face. Frances pretended not to notice. 'Douggie and I came down here for a wedding once. Do you remember the Adcocks? It was their daughter's wedding. She was barely nineteen. Their only child. The groom was a much older man. He was rather good-looking in a suntanned kind of way. I said to Douggie, "I hope he's not a bigamist."'

'What did Daddy say?' Vivienne asked. She split open the plastic bag that contained the potatoes and tipped them into a pan of water. She switched on the hob.

'"Unlikely. It's illegal." He never liked what he called "loose talk". But, you know, it was only ever a bit of fun. That's all it was. Those look very good potatoes. You don't scrape them? That's the modern way. It's all right. Roughage. But I can't say I really enjoy those little brown flaky bits. The flowers in the church were wonderful. All from the garden, though it was late in the year and everything was going over. Rosehips and eryngium and Japanese anemones. Kate Adcock always had a good garden. She must have worried about her daughter. Though there *is* something rather special about a very young bride. A young bride on her father's arm. A kind of freshness which is just not there later on when a woman knows all about ... ' Frances's voice trailed away.

'About what?' Vivienne asked. There were twelve sausages in the packet. She hoped that would be enough. 'Farm assured' it said on the label. She laid them out on the grill pan and switched on the electric grill. The smell of the cooking would find its way through the floorboards along with the ticking of the clock. Sausage smell wasn't too bad but cauliflower water wouldn't do. She would steam the cauliflower.

'They went to Singapore after they were married,' Frances said. 'That's the last we heard of them. Not that we were really close to the Adcocks. It's funny how you know so much about people's children and then it just stops. As if it all becomes dull. Or something goes wrong and people would rather not talk about it. I suppose something does, quite often, go wrong.'

'Grandchildren, though. They talk about grandchildren,' Vivienne said.

'Yes, they do. Though not as much as you might imagine. Older people can be very selfish. They talk about holidays and friends they've made on holidays whom you've never heard of. Bill and Annie and Raymond and Veronica. Then they meet friends of the friends and we have to hear all about that. Have you opened that bottle yet, darling? The church had some connection with Edward the Confessor, or was it Edward the Martyr? It had good glass, I remember. We could go on Sunday if you liked, darling; it's probably only a few miles from here. I wouldn't mind.'

'You don't go to church,' Bethany said from the far side of the kitchen.

Vivienne had almost forgotten her elder daughter was there, she had been so quiet. She was playing the good child, choosing cutlery for supper from the dresser drawer.

'Every now and then,' Frances said.

'You don't believe in God,' Bethany said.

'I most certainly do, Bethany,' Frances said. 'He's just not a personal friend of mine.'

Vivienne smiled brightly. 'I'd better go and see if Martha's all right. Just watch the sausages, would you, Mummy?'

'Leave her, darling. She'll be fine. I heard her skipping around up there a while ago. She'll come down when she's ready. We don't want any more hullabaloo,' Frances said.

There was an oval mirror on the dressing table with hinges either side. When Martha pushed it, it tilted. She caught different images: the floorboards with the fringed edge of the white bed cover; the leaves at the window and the triangles of sun between them. It was like taking pictures with a camera but the objects moved in the wind. Martha appeared not to be interested in her own reflection, nor in Vivienne who stood in the doorway watching her.

'Put your clothes back on, Martha, and come and have some supper. You like sausages and new potatoes,' Vivienne said.

The clock whirred and started to strike. It struck six times. Vivienne heard the clinks of plates being put in the oven to warm. Someone opened the door of the freezer. Martha walked round the room, touching the circlets of blue flowers on the wallpaper and touching twice when they coincided with the bumps of the uneven wall underneath. They could hear Bethany and Frances's voices coming up through the floorboards from the kitchen below, and the bees outside. Martha started to hum.

'It's a lovely room but it will still be here after supper,' Vivienne said. She could see why Martha liked it. The smell of the room, clean and damp – the green twining stems that squiggled in underneath the window frame. It was different from home. Vivienne had tossed a coin for the children's beds and tails had won, so Martha had chosen the bed on the left because the fringe on the bed cover was the same all the way round. The one on the other bed had some loops that were missing and some that hung down to the floor. Bethany said that the long loops could easily be cut with scissors but Martha said that wasn't true. The beds didn't belong to them. They belonged to Mr and Mrs Riggers who owned the cottage. You couldn't use scissors on other people's things. Vivienne had listened patiently, hoping to maintain the shallow peace. In the end, Martha had refused to come down. Vivienne understood. She, too, would have liked to remain up there. It would have been easier than lurching about, seeing different points of view, reconciling the generations. 'If you don't want to get dressed again, Martha, put your pyjamas on. They're in the top drawer,' she said.

'It's got funny handles.'

The drawer had two handles that were fastened with screws each side and the one on the right had a screw that didn't match the others. It was steel instead of brass and had a cross in the middle. Martha shuddered, backing away, as her mother opened the drawer.

'Come on, Martha. Put your arms up.' Vivienne held the pink shape out taut, as if it were on a washing line.

Martha held her arms straight up and Vivienne pulled the pyjama top down over them. Martha stepped into the trousers. 'Pyjamas are a defence,' she said.

'They certainly are,' Vivienne said.

5

In Sussex, the day lasted longer than in London – or the curtains were thinner. They were lightweight and filled out like clouds when the air moved through them. Then the shadows on the walls changed shape, flexing and overlapping. Although it was only ten o'clock, Vivienne had gone up to the bedroom. It had been the only way to bring the evening to an end. Frances loved to talk. She had a reservoir of memory and comment that had no regular outlet. Given a listener, the words gushed out as from an overflow pipe.

There was a gap between the two beds that was deep but not wide. On the other side of the divide the bed was empty, though Vivienne had turned down the covers. Vivienne imagined waking in the morning and seeing Richard with his face towards her, breathing, in sleep. It was years since they had slept in twin beds. A mistake in a hotel booking – and a mistake again now. She was sure that the cottage brochure had said two twins and a double. Then – whenever it was, she couldn't remember – they had both squeezed into the one bed, not wanting to be separate. What were the chances of that happening this weekend?

Although Richard would probably not turn up for another hour or two, Vivienne listened out for cars coming down the lane. They came every three to five minutes and the headlamps beamed through the curtains. She thought of Richard driving alone along the motorway – a long, grey, straight stretch between hills.

Vivienne felt she had changed in some way. She was like a picture that had slipped down behind the glass and was no longer parallel with the frame.

Between the time of the strange presentiment in Prayer Clinic and the telephone call to Kirsty Rivers, she had suspected a woman at the bottom of Richard's troubles. Without knowing, or guessing anything about her, she had existed. Then, when Kirsty Rivers told her to contact her brother Abe, the Woman became more elusive.

On her journey to Shoreditch, and particularly once Vivienne had left the main thoroughfare of Bishopsgate and started walking through the unfamiliar side streets, she began to be nervous. She put flesh on the alarming 'brother' who materialised from the old warehouse buildings. She considered turning back and ringing the number she had been given from a safer spot. But she kept going – all the time processing her recent concerns about Richard: the mental lapses, the unexplained latenesses, the malaise and the moodiness. Her mind swung back and forth, checking her husband's 'symptoms' against random information she had picked up from the media and which she had never thought would be relevant to her. She ranged through problems involving ex-colleagues with grudges, ex-employees with grudges, bent auditors, conmen and stuck, finally, somewhere quite improbable – the pendulum at a gravity-defying angle – say, ten to twelve. Richard had gone to Shoreditch to buy drugs.

Vivienne forced herself up the stairs of the building where Karumi was located, as if carrying her own body up a steep hill. The room at the top came as a surprise: the calm and airy interior, the beautiful Japanese teapots. Immediately, Vivienne put this mismatch down to her own lack of sophistication. And Abe himself, although different from the crook she was expecting, also made sense in the context of her misunderstanding. In real life he *would* be an engaging man in his twenties and not a shady-looking fellow in a hat. The white-coated Tariq, the lifestyle magazines and the books, with titles like *Look After Your Back*, all contributed to the upgrading of her database. The odd thing was that once Vivienne accepted that her suspicion was utterly off target – which happened by the end of her conversation with Abe – she didn't revert to her former innocence. She was aware that she wasn't wrong to bin off the old assumptions. Even though Abe was not a drug dealer and Karumi not the perfect front, they might have been. This was, she could see, how things were nowadays. Her mistake had been to lay the finger on Abe as an individual – not a type – and on her husband in any way whatsoever.

After she had said goodbye to Abe and closed the door of Karumi behind her, she stood in the cell-like lobby, looking back through the frosted internal window at the room she had just left. She caught a milky version of her own reflection staring from the window, the pale green of her suit an odd bronze colour, her sunglasses black patches off-centre on her head. She reached up to straighten them before summoning the lift that she had been too afraid to use on the way up. It came clanking and rattling through the shaft. When it juddered to a stop, she released the catch and pulled open the grille. The action caused the inner structure to wobble in the way of a jack-in-the-box attached to a spring. She stepped inside and, feeling suddenly nauseous, stepped out again, closing the grille with a clang that reverberated through the building. She started to walk down the stairs. At each new floor level her heels tapped across the metal platforms. She continued until she reached the ground floor, then paused for breath as the constant turning and descending had made her dizzy. She pressed the buzzer to exit and pushed open the door. She was back in the street. Her situation seemed to her suddenly neutral, wiped clean – as if she had arrived there, without volition, from nowhere. She stood for a few moments on the front step of the building, reorientating herself, then headed back to the main road. Her head spun from more than the stairs. She had never before been to this extraordinary part of London, nor to a sports injury treatment centre, nor felt so keyed up by a conversation as the one she had just had with Abe Rivers. She was tempted to stay longer in the area – to go into one of the cafés, or look for the chic East End shops that she had read about in the weekend papers. Relief put her in a strange mood. She perceived new worlds, flickering on and off, and wanted to drop by.

Going down the escalator at Liverpool Street Station – Vivienne seemed to have done nothing but descend – she realised that she wouldn't be able tell Richard anything, even though he was the person she most wanted to tell. When she asked him how his day had been and he, having told her, asked about hers, she would *not* be able to say that she had travelled to a sports injury treatment centre located somewhere between Bishopsgate and Shoreditch, in search of a man called Abe Rivers. Richard would never get to hear about Abe – who turned out to be rather attractive – or his poor sister, or the ins and outs of alternative religion. Unless she came out with the essence of the story – that her trust in Richard had wobbled and that she had gone through the contents of his desk – she wouldn't have the scope to discuss the by-products, nor to share her excitement with him.

As Vivienne stood on the crowded platform, waiting for a train to take her westwards, she felt desolate. For once, she had something riveting to talk to Richard about, something that would surprise him about her – but it was stronger than that. She had a feeling that her rediscovered 'trust' in him was a parody of what was really needed. She had a chance of a different outcome, if only she were able to speak. The black hole at the end of the platform that the train would rush out of seemed more like a vacuum – something that sucked people in. Vivienne felt the warm indrawing of air.

A car braked suddenly at the corner of the lane. Vivienne sat up, one of the straps of her silk nightdress sliding off her shoulder. She woke, panicking that she had lost the card inscribed with the feather. Then, seeing the curtains blowing over the window, she remembered where she was. The card had gone back into the wallet and she was in the country. She must have dozed off. She glanced at the empty white bed next to her. Richard still hadn't arrived. She considered getting up and looking out but she knew what she would see: the low wall filled with rock plants that divided the garden from the road, her own car backed against the farm gate opposite, the space next to it that she had left for Richard. She felt superstitious about seeing the unoccupied spot. She fell back on to the pillow.

Vivienne was still puzzled – though in a more objective way, since she was away from home – as to exactly why Richard had kept the card. She mused over it without reaching a conclusion – not in an anxious way, more as if it were some figure in the business plan that no one but the tax accountant understood. The clock whirred and struck the half-hour. It was still only half past ten. On impulse, she picked up her telephone from the bedside table and called Paula's number.

'Darling,' Paula said. 'I thought you were in Sussex. Wait a mo. I'm in the bath. I just need to dry off the phone.' Tapping sounds and odd knockings came down the line. 'Hello. I'm with you.'

'How was Normandy?'

'Terrific. But that's not why you're calling, is it, darling?'

'No,' Vivienne admitted.

'Sweetie,' Paula said.

'This is going to sound so ridiculous.'

'Tell me.'

'I found out, in a roundabout sort of way, that Richard was approached by a woman who tried to convert him to some esoteric cult,' Vivienne said. She kept her voice down, mindful of her mother and daughters in rooms across the landing.

'He saw her off, I hope.'

'Yes, of course.'

'Exactly what I'd expect of him. Hurrah! I must remember to ask him about it.'

'No. You mustn't. Promise, Paula. He doesn't like talking about it. You do promise, don't you?'

'Yes, of course.'

Vivienne paused. 'He kept her card with her number on.'

'And?'

'It's feeble of me. There's nothing at all to worry about. But I keep wondering *why*.'

'It was definitely a woman?'

'Yes.'

'Sure?'

'Well, she was called Kirsty. Oh, Paula, should I be worried?' Vivienne heard the slap of water against the side of the bath. 'Are you still there?'

'I can tell you exactly why he's kept the card,' Paula said. 'Sorry, I'm just getting out.'

Vivienne waited.

'It's obvious. He intends to pray for this person – Kirsty, did you say – and needs a reminder. Richard doesn't draw attention to himself. He's not a Pharisee, if I can put it like that. He doesn't sound off about his good deeds.'

'No, he doesn't. That's quite a good idea. You might be right.'

'I'm certainly right. Don't even think about it again, darling. God, if I suspected Hartley's business cards had hidden meanings I'd be a nervous wreck. Say your prayers and sleep tight.'

'Thank you, Paula.'

'Thank *you* for calling. I love to hear from you. Always.'

Vivienne replaced the phone on the bedside table and lay down again. She took a few deep breaths. Paula had succeeded in calming her – though it was the calm of the credulous. Vivienne found the idea that Richard might have been planning to pray for Kirsty Rivers oddly depressing. She preferred, for the moment, to delve around. Was the card with the feather a memento? Richard had had a blameless encounter with a misguided young woman and kept a token of it. Vivienne understood how such an action might arise – the safeguarding of a small but significant item that didn't fit normal life, a secret, in fact. She wondered whether possessing a secret, of a harmless but grown-up kind, made a person more interesting. She felt, for a second, quickened by the thought. Then – since the person was also herself – the flutter slowed and came to rest.

6

The same evening Richard had an early dinner appointment in the West End. On leaving the restaurant, he shook hands with his hosts, but instead of hailing a taxi or making his way back to a station, he started walking. Vivienne had already reached Sussex. She had left a message on his phone. Richard omitted to send one back, telling her that the dinner had ended. He passed through waves of din, as he looped round pavement drinkers lapping out from the pubs, then through calmer stretches, outside closed shops, where he was the only pedestrian. At Marylebone he saw the sign to the Underground but walked on, ignoring the trains that would have taken him home. He was heading in the direction of Paddington, where he hadn't set foot since January. It wasn't a part of London he had much call to go to.

He descended into the underpass beneath the Marylebone flyover and emerged in a different landscape. The Paddington Basin development had moved on in six months. All around were new buildings, some occupied, some empty – all lights blazing – and sites still under construction, wrapped up like parcels in what appeared to be stout polythene. Richard hadn't paid much attention to the precise state of the project back then – the snow had been a distraction – but he could tell that there were fewer gaps in the skyline, fewer holes in the ground. The wine bar, at the foot of the office block where his meeting had taken place, was below street level though there was no street – just a wide open space consisting of shallow concrete steps that went down and then up again. The doors of the wine bar slid apart as he approached.

He found a table in a quiet corner and sat down. The place was air-conditioned – a degree or so too cold – but Richard loosened his tie out of habit. He raised his hand to attract the attention of the waiter and ordered a glass of house red – his first drink of the evening. He had stuck to mineral water with dinner, conscious of the drive later on.

He had only spent one evening with the family that week. He had walked round the side of the house and called out hello. Martha had called back, but Bethany, with a bat outstretched, was concentrating on the ball that was about to leave Henka's hand. Richard, poised to clap, had changed the gesture to a two-handed wave when Bethany missed and the ball had sailed past into the pyracantha and stuck there. Whatever was arbitrary about the family – the tendency to spill out in unexpected directions – Henka firmed up. There was a frame – in this case the garden fence, partially concealed by shrubs, and the hours from the end of school until bedtime – which bounded them and from which there was no escape. The remains of the girls' supper and drinks lay on the slatted wooden table; their cardigans were draped over the bench. After homework and food, out came the supervised games. Bethany and Martha seemed united in a way that was hard to achieve when he and Vivienne were in charge. Watching the three of them – Martha, Bethany, Henka – at different stages of girlhood, Richard's thoughts seemed to fall in line. The opportunity to be depressed or troubled didn't arise. The minutes progressed in an orderly way.

He had entered the house through the back door. The shower was running upstairs, which meant Vivienne was back. Richard leafed through the pile of post that was lying on the kitchen table. He remained standing, automatically sorting, and making a pile of the flyers and junk mail. He slit open the envelopes that were addressed to him. Everything was familiar; the fruit in the big blue-and-white bowl, the biscuit tin covered in pink pigs, the girls' homework books with their names in their own particular scripts – Martha's large and erratic, Bethany's neat and square. Even the sun that sliced the table in half in the early evening, making half light, half shade, was domesticated – what he expected at that time of year. These seemed to be visible signs, not of a perfect family, necessarily, but one without loose ends – justified, in every sense of that word.

Richard took out the evening paper – dependable camouflage – and folded it back so that the quick crossword was in front of him. There was a cryptic equivalent that fitted into the same grid but his brain wasn't wired for it. He glanced at the impossible clues as if they were television shots of tribal people wearing bizarre headgear. He wasn't troubled that he couldn't relate to them. The waiter returned with the wine. Richard took a gulp and pulled a pen from the inside pocket of his jacket. Short sleep. Three letters. He thought for a moment and put in a word. Within five minutes he had finished the wine. He placed some cash on the table and returned the pen to his pocket. He abandoned the newspaper. The white squares of the crossword were empty – all but the three letters. Better to have left it blank since the word looked ridiculous. The waiter would think he was brain-dead. Richard left the bar and went in search of a taxi.

The direct route from the new development to the north-east of Paddington Station to the taxi queue to the east was only for the airborne – pigeons or seagulls. The railway tracks – an array of them – created an area of flattened, intransigent space that no one but track menders and train drivers negotiated. The planners had not yet devised a way round. Their new walkways by the Paddington Basin petered out and paths that weren't designated paths but gaps between old railway buildings had to be improvised. Richard had managed in the snow – and on this occasion, too, he found a way. He didn't know what he expected to achieve by retracing his January steps. There was the example of actors appearing at an earlier scene of crime, similarly dressed to the victim, to jog the memories of passers-by who might have been present on the day or night in question. Then there was the example – pre-dating mobile telephones – of getting separated from someone and going back to the place where you last remembered being with them – in the hope that they would do the same. Neither of these examples suited the case, but a fragment of each existed in Richard's mind. At least this was an authentic route, not delusional. Different from his peregrinations through Harrow-on-the-Hill, which had turned out to be based on a trick of the mind. He wondered how else he had been mistaken.

He was still struggling with the notion of Laura McDermott – music teacher, homeowner, possessor of an Egyptian-looking stone cat and a fine singing voice. He had been so convinced that he had found Abe's sister that even now he had difficulty giving up the idea. He had considered circumstances in which people weren't who they said they were, or had multiple names, but Laura McDermott had been so stalwartly herself – whatever she was called – there was no doubting her. She had an integrity that was palpable and showed no sign of turning slippery at the edges. Her eyes – guilelessly – seemed to search him out. Her hands had been less steady, fiddling with the bracelets and the clump of hair. Richard had found her attractive. She was rather too opinionated to live with comfortably but he wouldn't have minded taking part in a quick experiment – *mutatis mutandis* – in which he woke up next to her, or came home to her one evening. Would someone so forthright – such a fearless communicator – not be easier to talk to than Vivienne? He could imagine not exactly confiding in Laura McDermott – she wasn't the cosy type – but laying those things before her which he struggled to forget. Would he not, without writhing in acute mental pain, be able to look her in the eye and tell her what they were? Because, whatever her reaction, whether she somehow gave him absolution or alternatively showed him the door, *she* would be able to cope.

The alley that Richard was walking along came out by Paddington Station. He went up the sloping ramp that led to the platforms and crossed the station concourse. He passed commuters who waited in front of the departure board and those who had no intention of travelling – purple-faced drinkers and old topers with bedraggled yellow beards. They struck poses with their beer cans, looking as if they had grabbed the cans and ossified. Individual whoops and shouts rose up and echoed in the hollow arch of the roof – the emptiness of homegoing. Richard walked through the covered passage that led to Eastbourne Terrace and out to the taxi queue.

There were only half a dozen people waiting. The evening was fine – still light – and there were no obvious problems with the transport system. The line wasn't long enough to have reached the sign that said, 'QUEUING TIME APPROXIMATELY 8 MINUTES FROM THIS POINT'. Richard couldn't remember having noticed the information in January, nor the pinkish electric bulbs that hung from the underside of the station canopy. The dimensions of the place were also somehow different; the distance between the ground and the apex of the canopy – the relative position of the brick wall opposite. Did his lack of observation, on that winter night, mean that he was already in an unreal state, his feet frozen and his senses engaged by the man standing next to him? He felt stupid not knowing the answer. Over the last months the timescale of the episode seemed to have unravelled into moments so distinct that he could walk all round each one and examine it. But now he perceived unevenness.

He had, in a sense, lost Abe for a second time. Believing he knew where Abe lived had soothed him. He could go to the house in his thoughts. Richard half suspected that if he hadn't been so asinine as to force the issue by returning to

'Abe's' road, Abe would somehow still be there. By behaving like a stalker, even for half an hour, he had done Abe and his sister, Kirsty, out of a nice little property and himself out of a consoling fantasy.

He joined the queue. The couple ahead of him had their arms round each other. Richard shifted away, not wanting to be too close, and looked towards the turning point where the taxis swung round. He watched as one made the turn and approached down the slope – headlamps and orange 'for hire' sign on, engine modulating as it came to a stop. A man at the front of the queue climbed in. The people immediately behind moved up, but not the couple. They remained clasped together. The shuffling of their feet and their abrupt lurches to one side then the other made it an odd-looking embrace. The woman's hands were kneading the man's hips, plucking at his jeans. Richard moved back a step, but not fast or far enough, because the man broke away from the woman, like a ladder tipping over, and pitched into him. Richard held his balance against the sudden weight. The woman was left beating the air. 'Give it me,' she shrieked, the sound as unrestrained as rapture. She lunged at the man's pockets. Richard brushed himself down and retreated further. The people ahead in the line shoved closer together, leaving a space round the couple the width of a boxing ring. The woman grappled with the man, trying to prise her hand in to his jeans pocket. 'Tell me, then. Tell me. What's it say? She text you, didn't she?' she said. The woman got hold of the phone. The man yanked her arm behind her back. The woman screamed and carried on screaming. Richard looked away and then, within seconds, found himself watching again, mesmerised.

A taxi pulled up with another following close behind it. They swallowed up what remained of the queue and drove away, leaving Richard alone with the couple. The pair were locked together, scuffing the ground, swaying to and fro. The man grabbed the phone back and held it high above his head. The woman jumped up to reach it, bouncing on the balls of her feet, twisting and turning, like a dog after a ball.

Another taxi turned into Eastbourne Terrace. Richard watched with apprehension as it came down the ramp. He took a step forward, full of scruples about going out of turn. He cleared his throat. 'Do you two want this cab?' he said in a voice barely louder than normal volume, addressing the space below the straining arms. Why he bothered to speak or why – since his mouth opened – he couldn't speak up enough for the pair to hear him he didn't know. He might as well have been a talking fly – an inhibited talking fly.

The taxi juddered to a stop. The driver hooted. Richard eyed the couple and decided to chance securing it. Dodging round them, with a hope for inconspicuousness that recalled afternoons on the school playing field, he arrived at the passenger door. He reached for the handle, but at the moment his hand closed over it another stronger one folded over his. Richard kept momentary contact with the metal, then, as the immovable weight eased him to one side, he teetered and landed clumsily on his left elbow and knee. The wheel of the taxi, the sole of a large trainer and the edge of the kerb all swam together in front of him. An unpleasant, sweetish smell of tobacco and aftershave lingered. Richard heard a door slam and, in the few minutes it took to regain his balance, he saw the taxi's red tail lights at eye level – stationary, then receding.

'He's gone,' the woman said mildly. 'Bastard,' she added in the same neutral tone.

Richard scrabbled to his feet. He retrieved the briefcase that he had let go in the fall.

'You all right?' the woman asked. She brushed her hair out of her face and Richard could see that she was young, no more than a girl. Her expression was calm. She fished around in the bag that hung over her shoulder and took out a packet of cigarettes and a lighter. She offered the packet to Richard. 'Want one?'

'No thanks,' Richard said.

She lit the cigarette and took a drag on it, then held it in the V of two fingers, away from Richard. 'Do you know if there's a cash machine near here?' she asked.

'No, sorry.'

'I'll get the cab to stop off somewhere.'

They waited for about ten minutes. The girl finished her cigarette, leaning against the barrier between the pavement and the road. Richard walked up and down, testing out his left knee. The twinge that spread through the nerves, every time he landed on his left foot, was sometimes sharp, sometimes dull.

'Hurts, does it?' the girl asked.

'A bit.'

'Stop still. Give it a rest.'

After her advice, Richard felt he couldn't move. Although the girl wasn't paying him much attention he stood, balancing his weight evenly on his feet, turning his head from time to time towards Eastbourne Terrace to see if a taxi was coming. Surprisingly, the twinges stopped. He felt no pain. When the cab finally arrived Richard motioned towards it. 'That's yours.'

'Cheers,' the girl said.

Richard left Paddington soon afterwards. He collapsed in the seat of the cab, exhausted. He closed his eyes but remained awake throughout the journey. He felt as if he were following himself through the streets, a self who was approaching his own territory and knew the way as well as he knew his own breath in the night. But he lacked a sense of homecoming – perhaps because Vivienne and the girls were, for once, not at home.

At the bottom of Sudbury Hill Richard opened his eyes. Of course, the driver didn't stop. There was no snow on the road. The taxi carried on up and deposited Richard outside his door. Vivienne's car had gone. Richard's was in the garage. As soon as he had changed out of his suit he would drive down to Sussex.

7

At around midday on Saturday morning Abe left his room and careered down the front stairs two at a time, causing the hall light bulb to sway. His steps on the bare wood made echoes and the traffic hummed, but within itself the house was quiet. The two bicycles had gone, revealing scuff marks on the wall and drifts of dust that collected between the skirting board and the wheels. Luka had left – and Kirsty too, it seemed, on Declan's bike. There was a white envelope and a couple of flyers on the mat. Abe picked up the envelope, saw the giveaway window and dropped it on top of the other letters from the bank that were heaped in a pile. The pile was tall, heading for a tower. He gave it a kick and the letters scattered over the floor.

Abe went back upstairs. He finished the mug of tea he had made earlier and picked up the A4 notebook that was lying next to the swivel chair. Page one was torn out, but on the next page he had drawn a circle with lines radiating from it, beside which he had written 'sun disc'. Another page was full of scarabs. They were neat drawings with the divisions of the beetle form in the right places. Some of the creatures appeared to be smiling. Some had big eyes. On Thursday afternoon, after calling Richard's office, he had filled half the book. He had started to make notes on incorporating fitness into the Egyptian religion. Exercising for Osiris. Spin-offs had kept occurring to him. Government grants for combating the obesity epidemic. Backhanders from health clubs. He had fleetingly considered reintroducing the old religion to the Middle East and winning the Nobel Peace Prize, but had shied away from the trouble that that would involve. He hadn't planned to have Gloria as a partner in the enterprise, though he was sure that with more focus she could develop the business potential of her musical/spiritual interests. She was tough as a person, but not commercial and rarely left south London. Abe had broken into a cold sweat as he jotted down headings, worried that the competition had already got hold of his ideas and was at that very moment infiltrating the market. Yet, even as he had despaired of leading the field, the ideas had gone flat and he had remembered that no part of them was real.

His mania hadn't returned. He had called in sick on Friday. For the whole of the day he had sat around in his room, setting fire to small bits of paper in the ashtray. For the duration of the flame's flicker he felt alive but inevitably it died and then he was bored. He was also agitated. With him the two went together. Mood was stickiness, or rather, particles of stickiness that adhered to everything he thought and did, and which he tried to shake off. He envied people for whom trouble was a cloud or a blanket. Kirsty used mood as a hiding place. She made it cosy for herself, pretending she was perfect, martyring herself to borrowed goldfish. No, that wasn't fair. For a sister she was pretty faultless.

Abe dropped the notebook and crossed the room to put on some music. He needed to hear something new. He picked up a CD and put it in the player. 'Gesualdo RESPONSORIES' it said on the box. It was one that Declan had left behind before Christmas. The stack was still piled up in a corner. The music's edginess caught in his throat like the fumes from the traffic. Abe turned up the volume so that the sound went up through the roof and down to the basement. In Iverdale Road no one complained. Abe sat down in the swivel chair with the sleeve notes on his knee. *Spiritus quidem promptus est, caro autem infirma*. The spirit indeed is ready but the flesh is weak. The words seemed slick – on the one hand, on the other – but the music blew in a different direction, wanting to escape, still on the lookout. Carlo Gesualdo, Prince of Venosa, had discovered his wife having sex with another man and had organised her murder – and her lover's murder. A bit extreme, Abe thought. Luckily, Carlo had carried on with the composing.

Abe tilted the chair back, letting the sleeve notes slide to the floor. Church music had once been the business. Everyone had been in on it: family men like Bach, excitable types like Gesualdo. The band of sky that appeared above the opposite roofs was cloudless but Abe thought of a corporate golfing umbrella, rolled up, propped in the corner of a room. 'Are you all right?' was what he had wanted to say to Richard. On balance, the secretary's dependable voice had reassured him – the talk of a client meeting.

A woman on the top deck of a number 52 bus heard beautiful singing. She closed her eyes and listened. The traffic was stationary, waiting at the lights. Pull yourself together, she thought. There aren't angels on the bus. Tamsin Spira opened her eyes and lifted a strand of hair from her face with the self-conscious gesture of someone who used to be noticed. She glanced round to see if there was anyone behind with a leaking iPod. A man was asleep on the back seat. He had a grey hood pulled over his head but no trailing wires. A black kid across the aisle, half hidden behind a large sports bag, had ears empty as a baby's. There were no other passengers. Tamsin looked out of the window straight into a room. A young man was sitting in a huge mauve chair. The house was scruffy on the outside. All the houses along Iverdale Road were scruffy. Behind the mauve chair was a mirror that filled the wall. As the bus started to move, Tamsin caught sight of her reflection, framed by the bus window, staring out. Then, when she could no longer see herself, the singing stopped.